Sisters at War

June Elvin

Black Cat Publications

Black Cat Publications
41A Buckingham Place
Brighton
BN1 3PQ
Tel: 01273 776409

A CIP catalogue record for this book is available from the British Library.

Printed and bound in Great Britain.

ISBN 1 902320 21 2

Cover design by Caroline Sills.

About the Author

June Elvin was born in Streatham, London, the third of four daughters. Her father, disappointed in having so many daughters, decided to call her 'Michael'. Her mother, Margaret Flowerdew, was a well known writer, having written the bestseller 'The Lonely Road' using the family name of Flowerdew which dated back to the Domesday Book. Her grandfather was first violinist and conductor of the famous Hallé Orchestra.

Having such artistic parents, it was no wonder that June decided to be an actress at an early age. She was a child actress, starting at the age of twelve with the role of the small boy Tobias in 'Sweeney Todd' with the famous actor-manager Tod Slaughter. Success followed, and June was put under contract with Ealing Films, playing in 'Nicholas Nickleby', 'The Small Back Room', and 'Too Hot to Handle' with Jayne Mansfield. When recession hit the theatre in the eighties, June settled down to write 'Sisters at War', her first book, but the theatre called and she acted at the Edinburgh Festival and the Bath Festival as Kathy in 'Entertaining Mr Sloane'. She is currently appearing at the Westminster Theatre, having written the adaptation of Jane Austen's 'Pride and Prejudice' as a musical.

June was educated at Kerri School for Girls in Reigate, Surrey, and St Andrews School in Brighton. She has a son, Philip.

Foreword

I became interested in the Queen Alexandra nurses when I joined an Answering Service Company called AirCall, in the eighties. As a working actress, when unemployed, known as 'resting' in the theatrical profession, we have to work outside the profession in order to live. One or two famous actors and actresses, before they became well known, had started life in this way with the same company. This answering service included commercial and medical answering teams. The company employed people with good speaking voices, essential for telephone work.

One of my colleagues, who handled the medical department, was a lovely lady called Bridget O'Conner, who was an ex Q.A. From her, I learnt a tremendous amount about her experiences as a full Queen Alexandra Sister. The small council flat at the beginning of the story is where she lived, eking out a small salary and pension. With her true experiences and my imagination, I wrote 'Sisters at War'.

June Elvin

To Bridget O'Conner
Without whom this book would never have been written.

Chapter One

Prologue

Armistice Day 11th November 1984

There is a dull mist over London and the time is 10.00 a.m. Susan Jones tidies her small council flat off Commercial Road, London E.1., a dark basement apartment consisting of bed/sitting room and hall. Although it is tiny, it is sparse of furniture, the carpet is worn and sombre; a tiny black and white television sits on a small sideboard, it is shabby and scratched. The cloth covering a kitchen table is threadbare although neatly patched, the curtains are drooping and faded.

It is as if she had crammed all the meagre belongings of her lifetime into this tiny flat. War photographs are abundant of friends in the Services, and other nurses in uniform. Packing cases are piled high in the hall, and in the bed/sitting room. A single bed in the corner, hanging over it is a crucifix on the wall, and a rocking chair, sum up her possessions of this world.

It is sad, that this nurse, after a proud and zestful career she had had in the second World War, should end her life in a downhill battle, with nothing whatsoever to help her. She had given her life to the country, but had been abandoned in this lonely and impoverished way.

On the windowsill is a vase, and a few anemones; she picks them out of the vase, puts on her mackintosh, takes her umbrella and walks with difficulty to the door, takes the grey council lift to the bottom of this concrete building, and goes down the street from this East End slum.

At the bus stop are a few morning stragglers, she mounts the bus step and sits gazing out of the window to Hyde Park Corner. She then walks to the Royal Artillery Monument, and places the anemones at the foot of the statue of the unknown soldier, amongst all the other bright wreaths of poppies. Scrawled on a piece of paper are the words 'In loving memory of my darling Peter, who left me and this life so long ago. You are always with me.' This message is attached to the flowers with an elastic band.

The guns boom out the salute for the two minutes silence at 11 a.m. She closes her eyes, and her lips move in silent prayer. 'It won't be long now,' she murmurs. She opens her eyes and walks slowly across the road to the outside entrance of St George's Hospital, watching the nurses with avid interest as they scurry to and fro, either on duty or chatting to friends or helping the ambulance men, as they drive in with their patients. Some of them stop and wave to her, for they often see her standing there, a mountain of fat.

One young nurse comes over to her and sympathetically asks her, 'Are you alright? You don't look well.'

Susan looked at her young beauty and wished with all her heart that she was the same age. 'Yes, I'm alright,' then conversationally 'Today being Armistice Day, I've just put some flowers on the monument for the unknown soldier, for my Peter.'

'Did he die then?' the young nurse asked.

'Yes, at your Hospital, a long time ago, long before you were born.'

The young nurse put her hand on the old woman's shoulder. 'I'm so sorry,' she said. 'Goodbye, for now, see you soon, I expect,' she disappeared hurriedly up the steps to the Hospital.

Susan watched her go, then with a sigh she ambled away across the road, often stopping for breath. Impatient grey figures hustle and push into her, as she slowly trundles across the road again into St James Park. The day is particularly cold, damp and visibility is deteriorating. She sees a bench and gratefully sits easing her aching legs. From her carrier bag, she throws out lumps of bread, the birds come flying from all directions.

'I was one of them, you know,' she said to no one in particular. A huddled figure of a man sitting on the opposite side of the bench grunted. 'Yes,' she went on, 'I was one of those nurses, marching today by the Cenotaph. I belonged to the Queen Alexandra nurses. Can't do it now, of course, but then…' her voice faded, she was far away in her thoughts.

The man obviously didn't believe her, he looked her up and down. 'You a nurse, in yer dreams,' he grunted.

Susan rose abruptly shaking the crumbs from her skirt, 'I was a Sister and proud of it,' she said haughtily, 'Good afternoon.'

Susan started to walk away, when she caught sight of three nurses standing under the street light, on the opposite side of the road. They saw her, and beckoned to her excitedly.

The three were dressed in grey, bordered with red capes over grey dresses, with fine lawn headwear, the nurse's uniforms of the 1940s. She saw them many times now, in unexpected places, she didn't want to see them, she avoided them, if she could. Her guilt lay on her heavily.

Reluctantly she crossed over to them. They were laughing over a missed train, but whenever she tried to explain to them what had happened, they faded and disappeared in the yellow gloom. Susan carried on walking, down the Mall, passed Admiralty Arch, until she reached the entrance of Lyons Corner House.

Inside it was warm, and the glow of lights welcomed her.

'Wot yer want, luv?' the coloured woman asks her kindly.

'Cup of tea, please,' she wheezes, paying her 22p, and with her cup of tea in her hand, she settles down at an unoccupied table, languidly spooning sugar into the cup. Her mind went back to the early beginning of the war. It was the 23rd May. 1939. She started to reminisce. She liked reminiscing.

I was sitting in practically the same place as where I am now, in Lyons Corner House she chuckled to herself. The time had gone by so quickly, she could hardly fathom it, but the changes in life style were immense. She could only brood about the past, what else was there left in life for her? Susan didn't notice the rattle of teatrays, or casual conversations from others sitting nearby, she closed her mind to the din.

Sitting in the teahouse, quietly sipping the warm liquid, Susan became decidedly comfortable and sleepy, the lights and people faded. Susan saw herself, at the age of twenty four, dressed in the striped nurse's uniform, with sensible shoes and stockings, walking down Whitehall to the War Office. She smiled to herself as she remembered breathlessly entering a small room, having climbed many steps to get to the top floor, where behind the desk sat a Major of the Queen Alexandra's Imperial Military Nursing Service/Reserve, with a crown on her shoulder. Carefully noting down the whole conversation sat a further woman, with two pips on her shoulder.

After going through a few preliminary brief questions, the Major came to the important one. 'Are you prepared to travel anywhere, overseas perhaps?' The Major continued 'I must warn you. You could suffer starvation, and the possibility of extreme danger to yourself.' The Major looked down at the notes in front of her, 'Your records show that you are clear minded, quick and...' The Major allowed herself a faint smile to cross her otherwise austere features, 'unflappable.'

Susan replied in the sweet clear lilt of the Welsh voice 'Ma'am I am prepared to go wherever you choose to send me.'

Susan Jones was a Welsh girl, with a gentle musical voice. She had large blue eyes, strongly dimpled cheeks in a freckled face. Although dumpy in stature, she was always laughing and cheerful. She left the building, as if she were walking on air. She walked up Whitehall as if in a dream. Over to the Strand, when her eye caught a small cinema playing a French film and the inevitable news.

She decided to put off an hour or two before she went home. War was on everyone's lips, so she could catch up with the news, particularly as there was a possibility that she would be posted abroad. She was young, danger never occurred to her. She paid for a ticket, and was ushered to her seat by a somewhat bored usherette. Came the news, a cock crowing indicating Pathe News. Onto the screen came the great arena of Nuremberg. Standing there, under every conceivable batten of light, stood a diminutive figure in black, addressing an audience of thousands. The date January 30th 1939 swept into view. Hitler spoke in German with English subtitles 'Today, I shall act the prophet once again. If international Jewry, inside or outside of Europe, should succeed in thrusting the nations into a world war once again, then the result will not be the Bolshevization of the earth and with it the victory of Jewry, it will be the annihilation of the Jewish race in Europe.' The voice rose into a scream. Susan looked round at the audience, they were spellbound, in the same way as he mesmerised his audience in Nuremberg. At first the listeners in Nuremberg were quiet, then a roar welcomed his words, as he paused. Slowly a sinister soft note of Seig Heil swelled louder and louder in that great Arena. Came a flashback of the Fuhrer shaking hands with Neville Chamberlain, placating Hitler. Quick pictures followed instantaneously, with Chamberlain holding up his briefcase 'Peace in our time' followed by the Fuhrer kissing babies, shaking hands with blonde beauties and advocating the family life, with the voice of the newscaster in the background, 'The Fuhrer does not wish to solve the Danzig question by the use of force.' At this point the Fuhrer became agitated hitting the air with his fists, 'Me, you will never tire. I am determined to march on this path, I am convinced that we shall march faster than the others.'

The date 23rd of May 1939 swung onto the screen. Why, that is today, thought Susan. The voice became louder, 'Further successes can no longer be obtained without the shedding of blood. There is no question of sparing Poland, and we are left with the decision to attack Poland at the first opportunity.'

Susan came out of the cinema, her eyes blinking in the bright afternoon sun. She caught her train back to her parents' home on the outskirts of Swansea to await developments from her interview with the War Office.

Her father, Gareth Jones known as Garry to his friends, met her at the gate of their small semi detached house, accompanied by their sheepdog Sheppey. He was overjoyed to see her, asking her question after question, before she went upstairs to her bedroom to tidy her hair before tea.

She could hear her mother preparing cakes and biscuits in honour of the occasion. Susan felt a wave of happiness overcome her, she was with her parents, home and secure. She wondered to herself, why was she so keen to go abroad, to sever, may be for ever, her ties with her family. Her thirteen year old young sister, May, called Minnie because she preferred it, joined her, taking her case up to her bedroom. They rolled about on the bed together, so pleased to see each other. Susan looked round her room, nothing had been changed. Her old china dolls paraded on the chest of drawers including her favourite black doll. Looking out of the window, the garden and allotment tended so carefully by her father produced vegetables of every kind. The gate at the bottom of the garden led on to fields and meadows.

Her mother called her down to tea, and the family sat round the table as if there had been no time lapse, between now and her four years training as a nurse.

Gareth Jones looked at his daughter with great fondness. Susan was his favourite daughter, although he tried not to show any favouritism, but they had always been great pals. He would talk to her as if she had been his son, telling her all the gossip of the neighbourhood. But, not gossip in a womanly way, but about his friends and neighbours, and how they would all go to the pub on the green, and have a good sing song amidst many pints of beer. He never stopped talking about his daughter and the instruction she was given as a trainee nurse. Gareth Jones was a simple man, and had brought his daughters up strictly, to obey their parents, to observe the Sabbath, not to swear, or to wear makeup before the age of sixteen. Like most Welsh men he could sing, and had early ambitions of becoming an opera singer, but did not have enough musical knowledge; being the youngest of four children, the piano music lessons went to his elder brother, who never bothered to make use of his musical knowledge in later life. So, he settled, by joining the local church choir. He was now promoted to choir master, and rehearsed his singers twice a week, which gave him a wealth of satisfaction. People from far and near came to hear his Sunday hymns and concerts, throughout the week, in the village church hall. He felt his ambitions had been fulfilled in a different way. Fame and fortune was not for him, he might only have ended in the chorus anyway, he told himself.

September 3rd 1939 came and went. War had been declared between England and Germany. Russia had joined with Germany, but, nothing seemed so important to Susan any more, she was contented in the embrace of her family. Susan smiled at her mother as she was pouring tea. She loved her mother, Gwyneth, Gwen for short, because she was always happy and jolly. The blackest problems she could turn around, so they ended as trivialities; she had an answer for everything, in her soft lilting Welsh voice. Happiness shone around her. She was such an affectionate embracing person that you could, metaphorically speaking, warm your hands against the warmth she poured out to all and sundry. Children, strangers, animals, all came under her sympathetic wing. She had such a soft heart that people took advantage of her kindness but, although her purse seemed more empty than full, she took all in her stride, and shrugged off all bitterness and disappointments.

'What are we on this earth for?' she would say, 'if we cannot help each other?' and that was her answer to everything.

Gwyneth had recently taken courses on midwifery, passed all examinations, and was now a fully qualified midwife. Off she would ride on her bicycle, to various parts of the town. 'You can't stop the babies coming, popping out like jelly beans' and off she would go to another destination. Susan felt she had inherited this love of nursing from her mother, and, more than likely had given her the inspiration to start her on her career as a nurse.

There was so much harmony in this small semi-detached house that Susan, respecting her parents' unity, had secretly hoped the same happiness would happen in her future life, to find her soulmate, as obviously her parents had managed to do.

'Coming for a walk?' her father called, and they strolled through the gate, arm in arm down to the village on the outskirts of Swansea, with Minnie and Sheppey bouncing about between them.

Susan thought this idyllic life would never end, she had far distanced her professional life from her family life, and had honestly not given a thought to her future; therefore it came as quite a shock to them all when her papers came through from the War Office, just before Christmas. Her instructions were to travel to St Pancras station for disembarkation abroad.

At the beginning of March, 1940, Susan left her parents' home for Paddington station. This time, however, she is dressed in the full uniform of a Queen Alexandra Imperial Military Nurse, with a smart grey suit and tie, carrying a dark grey overcoat and case, with black stockings and shoes. She sat in the carriage, quietly, looking out of the window. The train chugs slowly into Paddington station. She sees Service men and women, bustling here and there. She follows a main stream of people, heading for the underground tube. Sandbags are stacked high, and the blackout is prevalent. There is plenty of fruit, vegetables and chocolates in the small station shops, and overhead are seen the silvery splodges of the defence of London air balloons.

Susan changed trains at Paddington station for Plymouth. The station was packed with Service personnel. The trains were late, and the platforms overflowing. A tea-urn lady was passing round tea, sandwiches and doughnuts.

'Cuppa tea, lady. Wot about a doughnut?'

'Thanks,' Susan accepted the tea and doughnut, and with her mouth full, she produced her ticket to the Collector, who greeted her with cheerful cockney humour, 'Berlin or bust. At 'em dearie,' he declared, with an admiring glance at her smart nurse's uniform.

Dig for Victory the posters urged her. Walls have ears the posters cautioned. She smiled at him, and left for her train which departed at noon on that spring afternoon. She found a seat on the overcrowded train, then pulling out a letter from her handbag she read Fourth Casualty Station, Plymouth. She closed her eyes, as the train plunged into a tunnel.

What did the future hold for her? she wondered, but in a few minutes she drifted into a fitful sleep.

Travelling by train in early wartime had to be seen to be believed. Slow, long and tedious, with no food or water. By the time the train, after many stops, had arrived at Plymouth, Susan was quite exhausted. She took down her case, and endeavoured to get off the train, but this was not as easy as she had first imagined.

She found she was completely locked in the 'in' section of the train, and found she could not get out of the train at all. She tried to attract attention, but no one noticed; she eventually found herself way down by Plymouth docks, in an engine shed. What a beginning for the career of an Officer of the Queen Alexandra nurses, she thought. Luckily she saw a little man coming along, a wheel tapper. She managed to attract his attention but he had no key to open the carriage door. Climbing out of the window was no easy task, at the same time trying to look dignified, with a tiny man underneath the window catching her as she fell. She then had to walk along the line to the Plymouth platform, very red in the face. There outside the station, fortunately, a car was waiting for her, to take her to the 4th Casualty Clearing Station.

Chapter Two

The Royal Victoria Infirmary stood like a sentinel over the town of Newcastle. A group of fresh faced nurses were listening intently to the grey haired Matron in her inauguration speech, congratulating them at their stage of transition. There was a garden party atmosphere in this ceremony of graduation. The parents of the girls with tears of admiration, formed the background, breaking into sporadic applause as each girl, individually, lined up to receive the passes of their Final Examinations.

After four years of practical training in the wards, they were in the proud position of being able to write S.R.N. after their names. They were now State Registered Nurses. Although the war between Germany and England had just been declared September 3rd 1939, the food situation at that time had no effect on the style of living. Tables were groaning with food, and almost every parent longed for a cup of tea, impatient for speeches to end.

Amongst the nurses, the dark Rachel Gelkop, with her brown luminous eyes, gazed trustfully at the Matron, who had the old fashioned idea that repeating the Hippocratic oath would instil into the minds of all nurses their dedication to their work.

The nurses joined in unison, like a prayer. 'I swear by Apollo, the healer, invoking all the Gods to be my witnesses, that I will fulfil this oath to the best of my ability and judgement.'

Each nurse repeated one line of the oath, and when it came to Rachel's turn, she recited fluently, 'The regiment I adopt shall be for the benefit of my patients, according to my ability and judgement, and not for their hurt or their wrong, though it be asked of me.' Rachel looked upwards at the clouds gathering for rain, and vowed quietly to herself; I lay my life down to help the sick and suffering.

There is a pause in the procedure, and with a loud burst of cymbals and drums, the band strikes up, 'Land of hope and glory,' the Sisters all cheer, throw their arms round each other, and join their parents for tea. Rachel does similarly; proudly and shyly she introduces her parents, of Polish origin, to her one or two special friends. She does not make friends easily, she is too reserved and her religion teaches her to be careful of friendship. Her family encircle her with their warmth and love. They were all determined to be at the ceremony, although they had little means, and were extremely poor. Nephews, nieces, aunts and cousins, hugged and kissed her as the formalities drew to a close.

Within six months, Rachel had applied and was accepted by the War Office as a likely candidate for the Queen Alexandra Imperial Nursing Service. On this bright February day in 1940, she came out of the Aldgate tube to show her family her new uniform of grey and red, which she was very proud to be wearing. As she emerged from the tube into the sunshine, she walked through the Flea Market on her way home, to where her parents lived, in Chapel Road, situated in the East End of London. In the market, the Cockney sparrows were still selling their wares, as usual, to the poor. She received many a cheery response, and many an admiring look, as she passed by their stalls. Rachel smiled back at them, some of whom she knew as a child, in the full knowledge of feeling great in her new uniform.

The further she walked, the meaner became the streets, one tumbling into the other, with little or no character, until she came to a small block of council flats. She ran down the steps into the basement flat, kissing the little metal box on the doorpost, holding passages from the Deuteronomy, and tapped gently on the door.

Her father answered the door. They were intensely poor, but her family, including cousins, aunts, uncles, nieces, and children, were all there to welcome her. The home has traditionally been open to all God's friends, these are the poor, the widowed, the orphans, the refugees, all of whom are mentioned in the book of Moses. And what a welcome they gave her. They drew her in, with exclamations of delight and admiration of her attractive uniform. She knelt down and kissed the children, who were falling excitedly all over her, like small puppy dogs.

From the kitchen she could smell the rice and lamb, being cooked by her mother for the Festival of the Passover, consisting of cakes of unleavened bread, a sauce called Charoseth made of almonds, raisins, apples and cinnamon, with a base of wine. Everywhere in this tiny hovel of a home was love.

Rachel looked at her mother and father with a new light; somehow every moment seemed precious to her now; whereas before she took the growing up into religion as part of the Jewish way of life, now it seemed to be the only way of life, and she wished she could stop the process of time and never move from this tiny home again, ever.

The service in the home began with the sanctification of the day, as at Sabbath, blessed by her father. 'Let all who are hungry come and eat,' he intoned, a cup of wine was handed round, and drunk by all of them. The candles were lit, and everyone sat round the table, as her mother served the meal of traditional lamb, mixed with herbs and rice, accompanied by several courses, in honour of the occasion, known as Sedar. Many neighbours and friends gathered round the table as well, apart from the family.

In the course of the evening, her father explained the exodus of the Jewish people from Egypt. Rachel loved this story and the children eagerly joined in, as everyone, individually, plays a role, whether raising a question or suggesting an answer. They would recite the story of the miracles, connected with the deliverance from Egypt, and from slavery, then join lustily singing the Hallel and traditional song; partaking of four cups of wine at intervals, with the appropriate benedictions, all this was obligatory. The ceremony lasted for two days, but would proceed to a further six days, and in those six days it was obligatory not to write or work. On the fourth day, a telegram was delivered telling Rachel to be ready for posting abroad.

Destiny intervened. Rachel arrived at the 4th Casualty Clearing Station, Plymouth, at the beginning of March, 1940.

Chapter Three

The last of the three friends was Teresa O'Conner. Teresa was born on a farm in County Wicklow. Her mother, Kate O'Conner, stared at the little bundle, and could not believe the girl belonged to her.

Her hair was black, her eyes were black, and she did not look like any member of the family that she knew. 'She must be the milkman's daughter,' joked her father, but he was very happy to cradle this small infant in his enormous arms.

Shamus O'Conner, her father, had been a sailor, having had some vague idea to save a little money so that when he called in every port, as was every sailor's wont, he would find the woman of his dreams, take her back to Ireland, buy a farm and settle down to farm life.

The idea of being a farmer appealed to him, with a wife to accommodate his needs and children by the hearth. That was his dream, but however hard he looked, he always ended with prostitutes, who easily took every penny he had saved. It was not until he returned to Dublin that he found Kate, working in a bar near the city centre. She had the attractive combination found in so many Irish people, of dark hair and blue eyes, and a way of looking under her eyes that captivated Shamus.

Every night he would be found, either sitting in a corner by the fire, watching her every movement, or else telling stories of his many adventures abroad to anybody willing to listen to his blather. It was not only blather, though, he had to exaggerate, otherwise his audience would soon get bored. It was all for the benefit of Kate, anyway. His stories fascinated her, and she would join in the gathering, after the pub had closed, and listen avidly to his overseas adventures.

Kate's folk, her mother and father, owned and ran a farm in County Wicklow, but the farm was getting too difficult for them to manage, so when Kate introduced Shamus to them, they were only too happy to make his acquaintance, in the hope that he would marry Kate and take the farm off their hands. This was perfect for Shamus, he couldn't believe his good luck, a pretty wife and a farm thrown in together; he intoned many 'Hail Mary's' for good measure.

He decided to invite his future father in law for a few jars or tots of good whisky at the nearest ale house round the corner, to get to know him, in case he should change his mind. This was an ideal moment, he thought, for the two women, Kate and her mother, to talk over arrangements for his forthcoming wedding, and it wouldn't cost him a penny.

The two men strode out, into the dark; it was only four p.m. but already thick clouds had gathered, rain being very likely. They came into the pub, warm and inviting and chose a seat in the parlour at the back, not to be overheard. Shamus suggested a hot punch for them both, to keep out the cold, as it were. Harry Flynn, his future father in law, was a man of few words, always wore heavy green tweeds, and thick farm boots. He came to the point quickly for whatever he said would be succinct.

'Kate's me only daughter, her happiness is all we require. We don't want her to marry a man who's only after what he can get. Marriage is for life,' he went on, 'and if you have any other ideas, forget it.'

'No,' said Shamus, 'I won't say I have been perfect, I've sewn my wild oats a bit, but who hasn't,' he observed quickly, seeing the look of dismay on the other's face, 'but I love your daughter, and I will work hard at making the farm a success.'

'Well, the farm's a wedding present for you both,' Harry grunted, 'but don't call on us if things go wrong. Me and the missus will be moving back to the old town, and the place will be all yours.'

To be quite honest, Harry was secretly glad that this young man had appeared from nowhere. Recently, the farm had been a great worry to him, as they had little help, only casual labourers, and new blood was just what was wanted.

Shamus O'Conner stood another round, the spirit was beginning to tell, and he was getting decidedly woosey, he glanced at Harry, to no effect, Harry had settled back in his chair, he had had his say, and there was no more to be said. Shamus made a few attempts for further conversation, which fell flat. He was just about to say that they had better go home, when Harry suggested 'one for the road' but, as he did not put his hand in his pocket, Shamus was quite pleased he only wanted half a bitter, he was steadily running out of money. They then wended their way back to the farm.

Kate's mother Margaret, a large lady, with bright red cheeks, told him to stay the night. 'You canna go home in this weather. Glory be to Jesus, canna you hear tha wind.'

He was ushered up to a small comfortable bedroom, and an oil lamp was placed by his bedside. After many 'good night son' from the family, he opened the window, looking out to a moonless night, hearing muffled farm noises above the wind, he muttered 'All mine, all mine.' He then got into his pyjamas, and fell asleep.

Kate and Shamus married, and in spite of the in-laws saying they wouldn't help financially, they never stopped helping the newly wed couple. Shamus fulfilled his promise, and they both worked hard to make the farm a success.

Along came little Teresa, their pride and joy. The little girl grew up, with curly blonde hair, dimpled cheeks, with the prettiest smile and blue eyes like her mother. She was crazy about animals, and would not allow her father to hurt or kill any of the cattle. They all had special names, and ran to her when she called them. To make ends meet, Shamus had to take some of the stock to the market, but he was careful not to let her know. She was puzzled when they could not be found, or when they never came when she called their names. She was asking her father what became of 'Cowslip' or 'Stella' and would cry if she didn't get an answer, so Shamus was obliged to buy further cows, to compensate for the missing ones.

On one occasion, when she was only three, Kate took her daughter shopping in the nearest village. Somehow she slipped out of her mother's hand while she was talking to a friend and disappeared. Kate was frantic, she ran round the village looking for her, along with many villagers. Eventually the little girl was discovered, having fallen down a few steps in a basement house, covered with flowers on both sides of the steps, cradling a butterfly in her hands. She wasn't at all frightened, and looking up at her mother, she said innocently, 'Look, Mummy, a 'flutter bye',' her own special word for the insect.

The family had two dogs, four cats, rabbits, goats, a peacock, which settled on the roof of the farmstead. If a friend or neighbour came in for a cup of tea, to partake of Kate's special cakes, he wouldn't be surprised if a nanny goat gave him a friendly butt in the rear; even a horse was known to look in, to receive a carrot or lump of sugar. Teresa's favourite was a little fox cub, called 'Dusty'. She adored him, and they were quite inseparable. There were, of course, mutterings from other farmers nearby, to do with their hens and geese, but, as Shamus said 'If they didn't see that their coops and hen houses were properly protected, it was their own fault.'

Kate had to be firm, though, with her small child, and made her look after the animals, care for them, attend to keeping them clean, and sheltered at night. At the age of five, Teresa O'Conner started school. Of course, Dusty had to come with her, but Mrs Flynn, the headmistress, said an emphatic 'No', she was not to bring Dusty to school, which resulted in tears, but, as Mrs Flynn explained, 'The little fox would be too much distraction for the other children.' Teresa, being a sensible child, would be sure to understand, and, as was explained to her, Dusty would be waiting for her, as soon as she returned from school.

Teresa grew up very quickly, one minute a small tot, now a teenager. She had the same little ways as her mother, looking under her eyebrows, glancing sideways, in another few years this habit would be considered coquettish.

When her mother grumbled, she liked to grumble herself, she being mainly the reciprocate of the peevish complaints. It was very grown up to grumble, so the animals were always being told their mistakes, but the animals always took it in their stride, as animals do.

At thirteen, she hung around the local vet's surgery, hoping they would spot her for any duty they didn't wish to do themselves. Scrubbing out cages, taking dogs for walks, grooming cats, horses, and, as it was all for nothing, the vets were only to pleased to oblige her.

It was not until Leonard Maguire, the vets surgeon, noticed how gently and expertly she handled the animals, that he said 'With those hands, you should become a nurse, that is your true vocation, have you ever thought about becoming a nurse?'

Teresa had not thought about becoming a nurse, but, that very evening, she announced to her parents that she was beginning to like the idea of becoming a nurse.

Five years later, in the winter of 1935, she committed herself to four years training as a nurse, at thirty six shillings a week. In Dublin, the nurses lived and studied in a nurses home, which also housed the classroom of the Preliminary Training School, whereby a six week course of instruction followed, before nursing started in earnest at the hospital. The war had been declared in England, conscription had been and gone in England, before Teresa volunteered to join the war effort, to go to France as a fully fledged QA.

Teresa found herself with a group of chatting nurses, staring at the board at the 4th Casualty Clearing Station, Plymouth.

Chapter Four

Susan's Story

The transformation from civilian nursing to the Services had begun. They were all Sisters now.

Susan found that her first task was to teach nursing to the men of the Territorials, for a couple of weeks, before she went abroad. At the reception area of the Casualty Clearing station, Susan joined a group of nurses round the notice board, which stated entire company to report this day 1700 hours.

Susan turned to the two nurses nearest to her from the group. They all talked excitedly together introducing themselves. Rachel Gelkop, tall, dark from the East End of London and Teresa O'Conner from County Wicklow, Ireland.

'Let's all try to keep together,' said Susan. She was fascinated by the cool grace of Rachel, tall and elegant. She looked down at her own, fat awkward little body, and sighed. She also liked the sincerity of Teresa. Susan needed good friends, and she felt an affection for these two immediately. This was a great day for the embarkation; although they were not allowed to know their destination, they imagined it must be France.

They wait with impatience, and then right on the dot, their Company Officer addresses them. 'You will be pleased to know,' his voice gruff with emotion, speaking to a sea of upturned faces beneath him, 'that the Sisters will be called upon to play one of the most important campaigns in this war. We embark at 8.00 hours in a day or two, need I add, this information be kept strictly secret.'

The three friends were issued kit, consisting of regulation men's khaki battle dress, trousers and jackets, heavy brown boots, groundsheet, a haversack containing a respirator, a water bottle, a gas mask, all of which had to be carried.

They were given a tin of concentrated meat, a bar of chocolate, a container of water purifying tablets, a French phrase book and small English/French dictionaries, with a packet of French francs.

It was the 10th of March, 1940. At last, they were on their way. They were also the delight of troops, whenever they saw the nurses in their strange clanking garb, either heaving themselves into the Hospital Convoy, or endeavouring to embark onto a Cross Channel Ferry. Wherever they went, they were met with good natured ribaldry from the troops, particularly when they caught sight of Sue, being the shortest and roundest, her tin hat bumping almost to the ground, struggling with gas mask and water bottle, 'Get off yer arse shorty' was her usual greeting amongst guffaws of laughter.

A day or two later, Susan Jones landed at Cherbourg. She was surprised to find no evidence of air raid precaution, no gas masks were carried by the civilians, an air of happiness and confidence prevailed, an almost hysterical gaiety pervaded the streets and shops. In fact, there was no evidence of any defence, no barbed wire or ack ack guns, no sandbags of any description, (as could be seen everywhere in Britain, especially in stations and seaports).

For much of the months that preceded the launching of the German Blitzkrieg against Holland, Belgium and Luxembourg, the atmosphere was of carnival variety 'laugh and be merry for tomorrow we die' was the order of the day. The French were determined to do just that, with lights blazing and no blackout at all. The French were certain that their famous Maginot line would stop any attack from any invader.

The Matron led the way to the waiting convoys with a determined look in her eyes. The crown on her shoulder eliminated any comment from the troops, as they helped the nurses into the trucks except for a 'Hold me' and 'nursy' and such remarks.

Susan Jones found herself taking up the rear of the convoy in the fifth truck, well marked with red crosses. They started on their bumpy journey. Through Caen, Rouen, straight to Amiens to the town of Abbeville, the French population cheering every truck, thrusting chocolates, cigarettes into her hands. They were so happy to see the British nurses, and they imagined the war would soon be over. 'Bon voyage a vous,' 'Bientot revenir' Sue shouted back to them.

They arrived at the British Military Hospital (the 11th Casualty Clearing Station) outside the town of Abbeville. As the trucks deposited the nurses, Matron again took the lead and marched the Sisters in line, with their neat uniforms and white gloves and white lawn square handkerchiefs on their heads, up to the door. Susan walked under the trees, bursting with spring leaves and buds, bright daffodils and tulips swaying in the warm breeze, in their well tended flower beds on each side of the pathway. Susan felt she was a million miles away from the war zone.

'You wouldn't know there was a war on, it's so peaceful,' said Susan turning to Teresa. 'Perhaps we'll be sent home shortly.'

Teresa answered optimistically 'Well let's hope we will get some swimming and sunbathing in beforehand.' She stopped suddenly in her tracks. 'Look at that.'

Out of a wooden horizon, like a vision glimpsed in a reverie, they stared in awe on the splendour of this fairy tale mansion, once a casino, now turned into a Hospital. It had almond pink stone, crowned by variations of intricate patterned roofing, bristling with turrets, gables, pinnacles and sculptured chimneys, with white stone abutments and white stone window surrounds. The beauty of the house took their breath away as they followed Matron to the door. There were many ambulances drawn up to the door, and quite a few on the grass verge under the trees, standing idly by.

Matron led the way through the oak door into reception, where the Hospital was all a bustle. The three nurses, including Rachel, had hoped secretly they would be kept together. Matron marched to the reception desk, and saluted smartly.

She was greeted by Stacey Scott, an Army nursing sister. She was a regular and had seen several years' service in the Middle East, but she was a very different regular from the norm. She was extremely sure of herself, had no time for rules, did and said exactly what she felt was right, and was afraid of no one. This, of course, sometimes made her enemies. She was quick to defend the weak and many a frightened junior nurse would be reassured under her protective wing.

She would have become top of her profession, but her own character held her back, and her dislike of rules and protocol were her undoing. She was brave, dedicated and good fun, a born leader. She was bordering on fifty, had one pip on her shoulder, which she pointed to whenever she felt she was losing an argument.

Matron was not used to the relaxed attitude of Stacey who only half saluted her, she showed her annoyance in her face, but Stacey did not notice her frown.

'Matron Hudson of the Queen Alexandra nurses,' she barked. 'We have done a roll call, and now they are all yours.'

Stacey looked over the many eager faces. 'How many?' she enquired.

'Two hundred,' was the answer.

'Gawd,' replied Stacey, 'O.K. you lot. Follow me.' All the nurses followed her as she ascended the marble staircase behind the reception desk. 'I will show you your quarters.'

She pointed out a quick resume of wards, kitchens, etc. Susan followed her, staring unbelievingly at the still opulent Casino. The Casino itself had been converted to a surgical ward, but they still came upon tinted mirrors, unexpected painted cherubs in the corners, sumptuous velvet curtains. The honeymoon suite was now an operating theatre. From the landing on both sides were further wards, the sisters quarters were one floor up. In the 600 bedded hotel were mobile x ray sections, Surgical Medical Wards, Pathology and Dental Sections.

Stacey Scott deposited the nurses into their quarters. The three friends were eternally grateful they had been kept together. As they started to unpack, Stacey popped her head round the corner, 'If you hurry up, nosh at 1800 hours,' she smiled at them encouragingly.

Life for all of them was very different from nursing in a civilian hospital. To begin with, there were no female patients. These were no nonsense wards, strictly clean and tidy, with every locker laid out parade fashion. Towel, soap, and shaving gear just right. Patients were kept lying in bed for quite a few weeks after an operation, and it was the Sisters' work to see that the patient was well looked after, apart from basic care.

Susan would be on her rounds at 7 a.m. organising the day staff for bed pans, breakfasts, diets, medicines etc. In those early days, the new wonder drug, Penicillin, was given in massive doses, by three hour injections. Also an antibiotic tablet called MB that left in its wake of depression.

Susan would collect all patients' charts of the previous night, and place them at the end of individual beds. Temperatures had to be taken every four hours, and there was the usual general activity round every bed. After breakfast, there were fresh dressings to be applied, and she took pride in setting up the trolleys. Every instrument had to be boiled and sterilised, and with her helpers, she set to work in the art of laying her trolley instruments. If they were touched, accidentally, the unfortunate person was given a thorough rating, and the task had to be started all over again.

Dust was a forbidden word. Wheels on the bed had to be turned a certain way, the windows opened allowing in the correct amount of air. Susan remembered one incident when Matron came thundering down on her because the wheels were not turned correctly. She became impatient with these small trivialities, and when asked by Matron what way the wheels should be turned, she answered 'Left…er right,' quickly correcting herself.

'Right, always right, you should know that by now, and don't leave the windows so wide open.'

Further trivialities thought Susan, as if one could correct the air that came through the window. It was just her luck that her patient Mr Turner, whose bed was by the window, started to cough.

'There, you see,' Matron rounded on her triumphantly, 'poor Mr Turner will catch his death of cold.' He probably coughed on purpose, Sue thought, but, although she felt she was picked on unmercifully by Matron, without realising it she was learning all the time.

Wards had to be in apple pie order before the rounds of the Commanding Officer. There was a very harmonious atmosphere between patients and Sisters. The Queen Alexandras, in their starched white veil caps, queened it happily, like untiring ceaseless butterflies, fluttering from bed to bed.

At noon lunch was served to patients, and the nurses took lunch in the ballroom/dining room at 12.30. This would mean not one minute later, otherwise, there was no lunch. Everyone sat in strict seniority round long tables and were served accordingly, and, as Teresa and Susan were the youngest of the unit, they were the last to receive their food, which was usually cold by the time it reached them.

'Just because I am the youngest,' said Teresa plaintively, 'my food is always cold, I shall have to complain,' but, as she didn't know who to complain to, so the situation remained the same, as ever.

All Sisters were called by their surname, it was always Sister Jones or Sister O'Conner, never first names. After lunch it was the same routine again, boil and sterilise, sterilise and boil. Finish off dressings. Mobilisation of new patients. The operating theatre never ceased and all patients had to be prepared for their operations, which meant stripping and gowning them, injecting and shaving them for theatre.

Then, there was tea to be prepared, and after tea, washing pressure elbows, bottoms, heels, shoulder blades. Supper at 6 p.m., bedpanning. Further boiling and sterilisations. Teeth at six to seven p.m. Another round before Susan could retire, exhausted but exhilarated. She loved her work, and her patients loved her.

By the third week, Susan, Teresa, Rachel and Stacey with several other sisters, were given survival training, to be aware and ready in case of encountering the enemy.

They were all ordered, in khaki battle dress, tin hats, and haversacks, to undertake a week's defence training, in open woods in the vicinity of the hospital.

Their teacher, a cheerful Regimental Sergeant Major Thompson, thought little of their efforts. The days started with the said Major Thompson putting the Sisters through their exercises. One exercise consisted of being upside down on a rope, swinging then, onto a high wall, scaling down on the other side. They all managed fairly successfully, until it came to Susan's turn.

'Next,' Thompson shouted. Susan came with a gallop, managed to get half way up the rope, then losing her hold, went splat into the mud. 'Oh dear, oh dear. What 'ave we 'ere? Name.'

Susan, spluttering with mud all over her face and uniform, managed to spit out her name 'Susan Jones Sir.'

'Got to pull ourselves together, 'aven't we? Can't 'ave our nursing officers letting us down, when we're fighting the enemy.'

'No, Sir,' gasped Susan struggling for breath as she had another shot at getting over the wall, only to fall back once again. Stacey and Rachel rushed to her rescue, between them, shoving her to the top of the wall. Susan yelled a short lived triumphant 'Hooray' as she assailed the highest point, only to topple over the other side.

'Oh dear, oh dear,' sighed the Sergeant Major.

They were taught how to catch fish with their bare hands, how to hunt and kill wild animals, how to defend themselves, butt, knee an assailant (even a sharp stiletto heel could be useful).

In the first two days, Susan fought against fatigue and exhaustion; she longed for the nights when they pitched their tents under the stars, built fires for warmth, cooked their hunt for that day, and then slipped into oblivion in their sleeping bags. She envied the way her friend Stacey quickly became accustomed to the whole exercise, and obviously enjoyed it. She would survive in any circumstance, she thought ruefully.

Sergeant Major Thompson made no bones about his admiration of Stacey, and made many a caustic remark about the difference of a Regular, and the raw recruits as he called the other sisters.

Back at the hospital, news began to filter through. The Germans had invaded the Low countries. A change came over the wards, slowly at first, and then gathering momentum, the casualties began to fill the wards.

At the same time (trying to assimilate the strict military discipline) Susan went about her normal duties, but she began to hear a sound she had never heard before, a hum of voices and a strange shuffling noise infiltrating the wards and down the corridors. Glancing through the windows, her alarm was confirmed, a slow stream of refugees, passing by the end of the well trimmed lawns, beyond the gates, supposedly travelling north, anywhere, maybe Boulogne or Calais; who knows. Dust filled the air this warm May day.

Nothing much happened for a week or so, the radio was blocked by interference, it was impossible to obtain British stations. The Sisters had to rely for their news from the patients or passers by, gossip, hearsay was rife, and fear was in the air. Like a pool with a pebble, the ever widening ripples penetrated the wards.

On the 19th of May 1940, the Germans were well into France. They boasted that Le Quentin and Le Cateau had fallen into German hands. How long before they reach Abbeville? was in everyone's thoughts. The river Meusse had easily been crossed by the Germans, simply because quite a few bridges had not been blown by the Allies.

The three nurses, along with others, were standing by the windows of the ward, staring out at the refugees streaming past the Hospital. Rachel, who could speak French fluently, was listening avidly to the radio pressed against her ear.

She relayed the news to the other nurses. They all looked at each other in terror. Teresa burst into tears. Susan put her arm round her, comfortingly, they both hugged each other, spontaneously.

Susan whispered 'We'll be ready at a moment's notice. When we are evacuated we'll have our bags packed and ready to go.'

Teresa looked at her, the tears rolling down her face. 'Shall we get packed now?' she asked.

'No, not now,' said Susan, catching sight of Matron, raging down on them.

'What on earth are you nurses snivelling about? What an example to the patients,' said Matron angrily.

'But, we're scared,' said Teresa, pathetically.

'Nonsense,' was the answer, 'alarm and despondency are forbidden in the wards, Gelkop and O'Conner get on with your duties, at once.' The two nurses scurried back to their wards. Matron looked at Susan. 'Come here, my dear,' she said more kindly, looking into her eyes, 'I expect you, as senior Sister, to be an example to the others. Your courage is what they are looking for, what they will look up to; do not let me down, I am relying on you.'

Susan could only mumble, 'Of course, Matron.' She was overjoyed, she had been singled out to be an example to the others. Never in her short life had she been so privileged, in fact, she had been mostly overlooked by relatives and acquaintances, as a rather dumpy, non noticeable. She drew herself up to her full four foot, ten inches height, and raced back to her ward.

The casualties filling the ward were terribly wounded, mainly burns and gunshot wounds. One young man, a piper in his regiment, informed them that his battalion had all but been wiped out. He lasted for a few hours, but died the same night.

The three sisters, along with doctors and surgeons, worked ceaselessly, cutting away blood soaked uniforms, replacing dressings over gaping wounds, administering morphia, which gave a temporary release of pain. The ward was packed to overflowing.

Susan was glad of her four years training, her hands were soft and gentle as she went about her grim tasks. Her twelve hour stint became more and more pressurised, but this is what it is all about, she thought, to help those who cannot help themselves.

Teresa interrupted her thoughts. 'It's all very well for Matron, she doesn't have to work like us. As long as our aprons are changed every minute of the day, crisp, white and starched, looking like little white angels, she's quite happy.'

Susan smiled at her. 'Come on, don't give up, get yourself a cup of tea, you'll feel better.'

Teresa grumbled 'I'm sick, tired and fed up, there's no end to all this.' Teresa never stopped grumbling.

'They will have to evacuate,' said Susan, 'they must evacuate.'

The three nurses packed their trunks secretly, not before time, because they were the only nurses to get their luggage out, the rest had to be abandoned. On that same fateful day, news came swiftly in the form of a local civilian who had obviously panicked, an elderly relation of one of the French wounded. She ran into the ward and tried to force this very ill young man out of his bed. 'Dress quickly, you must leave,' she panted. 'The Germans are coming,' then she turned to the rest of the ward. 'The Germans are coming,' she repeated.

'Stop it, stop it immediately,' Susan commanded, trying to prevent pandemonium in the ward, but the woman would not be stopped. She ran round, like a headless chicken, screaming hysterically.

Matron appeared from nowhere. 'Jones, what is this woman doing running round in this way?'

The woman seized on Matron. 'You must leave immediately. Why are you standing there? The Germans are coming.'

Matron stepped forward, slapping the woman hard on her face, 'Stop the noise, immediately. I'm sorry, but you are upsetting the ward.' The woman dissolved into tears. Susan did her best to comfort her.

Taking no notice, Matron turned to the rest of the ward. 'We will be evacuating, as soon as possible, with the help of the Military; every patient able to walk will help with the evacuation, so with your help we will soon be back in England.' A cheer went round the ward. 'Good old Matron.'

The evacuation went smoothly, but it was impossible for everyone to leave. The wounded were transferred by ambulance to be transported to an awaiting Red Cross train at Abbeville station, that was the general idea. The wounded went ahead with medical orderlies to attend to their transportation; the Sisters, medical personnel etc, followed in ambulances and trucks.

Slowly the procession turned into the roads. It was impossible to move. The roads were littered with every kind of vehicle imaginable, old crocks, cars of every description (many having broken down were steaming by the roadside), carts, bicycles, all literally filled with immense freights of people and possessions. The refugees walked painfully and slowly, their feet blistered and bleeding, they had come a long distance. Rich and poor alike were struggling to get away, anywhere, away from the Germans.

We will never get there, thought Susan. She was travelling on the last truck of the convoy, with her were Rachel, Teresa and Stacey, incongruous in their starched aprons. Thick dust arose as the pitiful crowd surged forward.

An hour must have gone by, maybe two or three. People too exhausted to move were lying by the roadside. Now and then, they would put their arms out pathetically for help from the Red Cross ambulances.

'Should we help them?' asked Rachel.

'No,' answered Stacey, 'otherwise they will all want help, and then there will be no medicine for our own patients.'

'How long have we been here?' said Susan.

The truck moved a few yards, and then abruptly stopped again.

'Three hours, at least,' said Rachel.

'I'm famished, what would I do for sausages and mash, with mushy peas, right now,' sighed Susan.

'Give yer all,' said a nurse.

'What you haven't got,' said another nurse laughing. This was enough to set them all laughing.

'Very funny,' said Susan, who laughed in spite of herself.

At last they arrived at the station, although it was barely a few kilometres from the hospital; there the same scene recurred but this time infinitely worse. The crowd had been at the station for three days, kept there by rumours that a train would arrive shortly. When the hospital train arrived, the crowd surged forward, determined to get on it come what may, but they were repulsed by the troops with machine guns at the ready. Pandemonium set in. The ambulance convoy struggled to get the wounded on the train and to keep back the panic stricken crowd.

The four nurses had disembarked from their truck and were making tracks towards the train, when a woman clutching two small children cried to them, 'Please, my children they will die. Please help me, take my children, do not worry about me,' the woman insisted in a mixture of English and French, 'I am finished,' she sank by the roadside, 'I can go no further.'

Stacey looked at Rachel and Teresa in consternation, but immediately took command, as was her wont. Spying a gendarme, she called out to him and he forced his way over to her, the sweat falling down his face.

'These children are dying from starvation, you must find them something to eat,' then turning to Susan she added, 'We will find them something to eat. You stay and help the others onto the train, we will help the kids,' and commandeering Rachel and Teresa, she said to the gendarme 'There is milk and food in shops over there,' pointing to the shops which had been locked and shuttered, by their hurriedly departing owners.

'You cannot have this food,' protested the policeman.

'I don't care,' said Stacey, 'the Red Cross can requisition anything they like in an emergency.'

With that, she pushed her way to the shop, followed by the children and many curious onlookers. Stacey picked out one or two strong men from the crowd, one of whom willingly put his shoulder to the door and within minutes, amid a shower of dust, it burst open. The crowd, on to a good thing, followed. The shelves were bared almost immediately, as the people shoved and grabbed anything they could get their hands on, but not before Rachel and Stacey had seen that the children would be fed with good condensed milk and biscuits. When the shop had been stripped of everything in sight, they ransacked the next one. Someone shouted 'Look out, a raid.'

About forty bombers flew over Abbeville and the station. They were accompanied by a single plane, flying low, indiscriminately machine gunning the population below. The Nazis were savage fighters, relying on the old idea of frightening the enemy with howls and screams. All along the hundred mile front this idea was put into effect, so as to disconcert the Allies and refugees, alike. The plane had been fitted with a hideous noise maker on its nose, to terrify the wretched people about to be bombed underneath.

The plane roared as it dived at the station. Stacey, Rachel, Teresa and the children took cover as well as they could under the empty shop shelves. In no time the station was ablaze.

Leaving the children in the care of the gendarme, the three nurses fought their way through the carnage of bodies, the screams and cries, back to the ambulance train they assumed was still awaiting them. They stared in consternation. The train had gone, their absence had not been noticed in the confusion. The three nurses stared at each other in disbelief.

Teresa said, uncertainly 'The train has gone. What do we do now?'

'Oh, my God!' said Rachel.

'They could have waited for us,' grumbled Teresa.

Stacey turned on her angrily. 'Don't be stupid. Do you realise what danger we are in? All we can do is go back to the hospital.'

Chapter Five

Susan, having left the three nurses in their bid to find food for the children, struggled back through the crowds, forcing her way back to the train. Immediately, she was embroiled in getting the wounded onto the train, seeing they were comfortably settled into the bunks on each side of the carriage. The Hospital staff were concerned in getting the patients and equipment onto the train, and the Military were equally as anxious in seeing the train leave, as quickly as possible, before the track was bombed, which would have made their escape out of the question.

The train shuddered with much blowing of steam, jerked, and slowly started, and in no time they were off, gathering speed as they went. An air raid was taking place as they left. Looking back, Susan could still see the blazing town with thick smoke rising to the skies. They were now speeding past the Somme river, congested with refugees, civilians, and troops, out into the open country where peace and sunshine poured down on the cornfields. A German plane flew low beside them, spattering the train with bullets, but causing no casualties.

If only we could have stayed to help this country and their people, thought Sue, but such thoughts were brusquely dismissed when they drew into Boulogne, they were obviously due to go back to England.

They unloaded the patients quickly and efficiently as the train was urgently needed for further evacuations, but when they arrived at the quay side, to their horror there was not a ship in sight. They were at the mercy of the enemy, in full view, with no shelter, very little food and practically no water. Susan ran from patient to patient, comforting and reassuring them, but she could not dismiss the nagging doubt that maybe they would not be rescued.

Suddenly an old tramp barge, used mainly for coal, glided silently into the harbour. The Military immediately seized the boat, and the patients were wheeled onto it. The more seriously ill, emergency patients were put on the lower deck, and those who could walk on the main deck.

Matron looked round the barge, disgustedly. 'Now Sisters,' she said, 'this boat is extremely dirty. Even so, we shall expect you to have starched aprons, and gloves that are clean and white. It is essential that your appearance is correct when we arrive at Southampton.'

'Oh , really, white gloves on a coal barge,' complained Sue to the others. 'How ridiculous can you get.' However, they all did as they were told.

She began to worry about the other three nurses. She had not seen them since the departure of the train. At first, she presumed, they were on the train looking after patients in other carriages, but why had she not seen them? She realised guiltily that she had been so engrossed in her patients, she had forgotten all about them. She decided the only thing to do was to report their absence to the Matron, which she should have done immediately when she first noticed they were not on the train.

Matron was most put out, as she herself had not noticed this fact; she had also been too concerned about the welfare of the wounded and their transportation to notice the whereabouts of her nurses. 'They should be concerned only with their responsibilities,' she said crossly. She reported the fact of the missing nurses to the Military, who had escorted the whole operation from Abbeville hospital.

'Stacey Scott is a sensible mature nurse with a wealth of experience, she will know how to handle the situation,' the Major reflected. 'She will obviously go back to the Hospital, and we will evacuate them, and the few patients that were left, as soon as possible. Leave your worries with us,' he assured her.

When Susan heard this news, she could not contain her concern.

At last, the barge was fully loaded with equipment and casualties, the intention being to slip away as soon as it became dark. All eyes anxiously scanned the skies. There was no other ship in sight, and in fact, as it was learned later, the barge was the last sailing vessel to leave until the war was over. They had become fearful that the bombing would commence, and, as they were the only object visible, they were desperately vulnerable in that harbour. There were no red cross marks on the barge, obviously, until one bright nurse suggested they should turn their cloaks inside out, the linings of which were red, and would denote a cross. This they hurriedly carried out, although they were doubtful of the success of the operation.

'If they want to bomb, they will bomb,' one of the patients remarked gloomily.

Every nurse had bought a little bottle of champagne when they first landed in France, to take home with them. At last, the long afternoon faded to dusk, and they slid away under the cover of a moonless night. The barge had no water, and someone said 'If we run out of water, we will know what to do, as long as there is enough for the patients.' By the time they arrived at Southampton every bottle of champagne was empty.

Matron lined the nurses up in the early morning. Every nurse had to show spotless gloves, spotless white starched aprons, even though they had just emerged from a coal barge.

'As long as you look respectable in front of the other forces,' Matron said firmly. Dirty gloves and aprons were hurriedly thrown aside, starched aprons, caps, gloves were quickly adorned, but even the stern eye of Matron had no effect on the giggling nurses, in their efforts to form an orderly line before they disembarked.

Susan came out of her reveries abruptly, as a coloured Asian woman gave a listless wipe down of her table with a damp cloth. Susan glanced at her watch, goodness, she had been there for nearly two hours. It was now 2.30 p.m. in the afternoon of 1984. She had the whole of the afternoon to fill in the hours of an empty day, before she trailed home. She heaved her ample self out of the chair, and folded the empty carrier bag neatly into her handbag, she then wandered out of the cafe.

The afternoon had brightened into an Indian summer's day, cold but sunny. She crossed the road down to Trafalgar Square, and sat on a bench close to the parapet encircling the fountain.

She gazed at the fine spray shooting out of the fishes mouth in a never ending stream of water. The scene was the same, some forty years ago, she mused. There were the same pigeons, the street vendors selling peanuts to the many unsuspecting visitors, who, whilst feeding the pigeons, were being snapped by the photographers. The birds perched on the arms or even the heads of the feeder. Prices were quickly exchanged and extracted.

Susan looked on this scene, as she remembered forty four years ago. It was here, in this exact place, that her photograph was being taken feeding the pigeons.

She was young and attractive then, she sighed, as she saw herself in her Queen Alexandra's uniform, laughing for the photographer. Suddenly, she remembered, a young naval officer had been standing by, watching this procedure. Swiftly he grabbed flowers from a vendor and with a bow offered the flowers to her. She graciously accepted on this warm summer day, on the 6th September, 1940.

The street photographer is delighted. 'Ere mate, you step in the frame and present the flowers to the lady, as you just did, it will make a luverly picture,' and he proceeded to take the picture of the two young people together.

The guns are booming at an aerial dog fight taking place above them, and all civilians are watching, and talking excitedly, and pointing at the vapour trails discharged by the aircraft, which form intricate patterns in the sky, like an abstract painting.

The Germans were now in full occupation of the north of France, their success was startling and overwhelming, no one could believe it; as yet the full horror of war had not had much effect on the British people, they went about their normal business, despite all the signs of impending danger. Pubs were doing fantastic business, and cinemas and theatres were full in this phoney war. Buses and trams were running in an orderly fashion, with no destination boards. Travelling in London was particularly difficult, as landmarks were hidden by sandbags, and signposts had been taken down. A newspaper vendor sitting nearby gave the aerial contest a sporting flavour, by repeating the aircraft losses in the same way as a cricket score.

Susan chuckled to herself. What wonderful days they had together, this young blonde naval officer, Peter Francis, who attracted her so much. She recalled turning away to buy a newspaper, only to find he had followed her, determined not to lose sight of her.

'Do you know London, because if not, can I be your escort? Maybe you would like lunch with me?'

She remembered smiling, 'I would love to find out about London with you.' They caught a number nine bus up the Strand, where they dined at the famous Dickensian restaurant 'The Cock' where Dickens and his friends had dined many years before. After an enjoyable lunch, where they had exchanged the kind of conversation, amusing, flirtatious, bantering, that has ensued from the beginning of time in all sorts of languages, when a man is attracted to a woman and does not want to lose her.

Peter Francis is a young man and had not as yet engaged in any battles, and did not know the full implication of war. He is a little brash in his insecurity and small knowledge of women, but extremely charming and sensitive, and through their conversation, they find they are both unattached.

She saw herself going into the cloakroom to adjust her hair and make up, telling herself at the same time, to be careful. After all, she had been a mere pick up. Still, she shrugged, she was young, why not have as much fun as she could get. In those days, people made their minds up quickly, fearful their lives could be ended within days, by bombs, shrapnel, bullets, all in aid of the war effort.

Susan came back to where he was sitting, paying the bill. 'Where to now?' she laughed.

'We'll take a taxi.' Outside the restaurant he hired a taxi.

'Where to, Guv,' the taxi driver enquired.

'Anywhere, everywhere, I need to show the young lady London town.'

They passed theatreland in the Strand, St Paul's Cathedral, the Tower of London. His knowledge of London was profound, he knew his history, and turned his information into an exciting tour. Peter pointed out churches designed by Christopher Wren, back to the Houses of Parliament where Charles the First stood in front of the Assembly condemned to death.

Most of the time, however, he just wanted to put his arms round her and smother her with passion, after all, he only had two days before he joined his ship, he thought ruefully.

Eventually he paid the driver, and they strolled through Regents Park. They walked over a bridge and leant on the railing overlooking the Serpentine. They watched the cheeky ducks, and the appearance of two graceful swans gliding peacefully under the bridge.

'They mate for life,' said Peter, 'If one dies, so does the other, that's how it should be. Real love, not the hopping in and out of bed as humans indulge in.'

'Do you believe in real love. I mean, at first sight?' said Susan.

'Yes,' he replied, 'I believe in soul mates, but, not always found in a lifespan.'

'Peter,' Susan paused, making up her mind, 'I think I can trust and confide in you.'

'Try me,' he replied, with his infectious grin.

'I have been worried for months,' said Susan, 'I have no one I can talk to, who I can trust. You see, since March, I have been nursing in France, but, only after a few weeks, we were evacuated back to England in May, because of the invasion of the German army. We had to get out pretty quickly, as you can imagine, but in the rush and confusion of getting the wounded onto the train, I did not report that three of my friends, I mean our nursing team, were not on the train. To tell you the truth, I had not even noticed their absence. When the train arrived at Boulogne, and I realised they were definitely not on the train, I plucked up courage and told our Matron. To this day I have not heard from them since, it is as if they had never existed.'

'Oh! Don't worry,' he reassured her, 'people go missing all the time. It's the war, but, usually they turn up. Have you rung the War Office?'

'Oh, yes, almost every day, they must be fed up with me by now.'

'I'm sure they will turn up, have faith,' he said, slipping his arm round her shoulders, and giving her a little hug, 'Try not to worry. Shall we have tea?' He spied a small cafe by the lake.

The warm hazy afternoon dwindled away and they ended the evening by dancing and dining at the Trocadero. They emerged in the early morning, dawn was breaking when he hailed a taxi to take her back to her room. He had an inexplicable longing not to let her go, asking her to come to his hotel for lunch the next day. He was staying in a small hotel near Victoria station. The warm weather continued, with the 7th of September dawning clear and bright, not a cloud in the blue sky.

Susan arrived at his hotel in Victoria, where he met her in the foyer, they kissed each other rapturously, then he went to the reception to sign her in, as his wife.

The receptionist, who combined the work of typist and telephonist, was a middle aged woman of hawklike demeanour. The hotel comprised of two boarding houses joined together, and Peter had a room on the second floor. It was entirely run by women, as the porter and the chef had long ago been called up.

Where before they kept to a light flirtatious tone, now he had become more intense, and he told her that he had fallen crazily in love with her, asking her if she would marry him, as soon as he gets his next leave, or even before his present leave is over, if he could find a priest or registry office to perform the ceremony. Hardly sensible though, as the very next day he would have to join his ship, but he wanted to make use of every moment they could have together. There was a great possibility in wartime that if they parted they may never see each other again.

Susan, in her turn, is also mesmerised and half in love with him. He tells her that he has a present for her, a very private gift, but would prefer to show it to her in the privacy of his room, away from the curiosity of other people. She made a small protest, easily overcome by him, and taking her to the lift, he shouted to the receptionist to send a bottle of champagne to his room.

Susan kept her left hand under the cape, as the suspicious eyes darted to look for her wedding ring. In those days, men and women had to sign a Register in every hotel, so that the Ministry of Defence could keep an eye on all foreigners in the British Isles. When Susan went to sign the Register as Mrs Peter Francis (nowadays it is not important whether a person is married or not) she only knew her boyfriend as Peter. She coloured furiously at having to make an excuse to ask him in a whisper, what was his second name. She then nonchalantly returned to sign the register, deciding to ignore the acid remark of the receptionist, 'Madam has no luggage?' although it made her feel very uncomfortable, as she took the lift to the second floor with Peter.

The champagne arrived, sent up by the old retainer, with two glasses. Peter filled her glass, and together they stood in front of a somewhat dusty mirror, and toasted each other. At the same time he went to his drawer, and taking a small box out of the drawer, he placed a diamond ring on her third finger.

'To you, my darling wife,' he said. He had bought the ring that morning. 'In the sight of God, we are already married.' He overcame all qualms and protestations by lifting her in his arms, placing her on the bed, and delicately he began to take off her uniform, in readiness of making love to her.

Susan was swept off her feet by this handsome stranger, and when he began to kiss her mouth, pushing it open with his tongue, she could no longer resist the heady temptation, or the flame that spread through her, her compliance was complete. His tongue darted in all directions, seizing all crevices, taking her nipples, hardened by desire. He had opened her, like a flower, she was now ready for his penetration. With no further compunction he pushed into her, taking her, he would not be denied.

Clasped in each other's arms, they made love through the afternoon. The air raid warning sounds, but as London had had many such warnings, they chose to ignore it. It did not matter to them.

Nothing like it had been seen before. On the afternoon of September 7th, 1940, the sky was blackened with aircraft as three hundred bombers and six hundred fighters amassed in two huge waves in France. This massive air Armada, twenty miles wide, was on the way across the channel, to attack the biggest target in the world LONDON.

With many of our fighters in defensive positions, the way to London was clear. Remorselessly the bombers droned into London where, in formation after formation, they dropped three hundred tons of high explosive bombs. Soon hundreds of fires were raging, houses collapsing like packs of cards. 842 civilians were to die, and another two thousand eight hundred were seriously injured.

Peter and Susan stared at each other aghast, as suddenly this darkened room is fired by the reflection of a thousand raging flames, the windows smashed in and the glass shattered onto their bed. Struggling into their uniforms, he shouted to her that he would go ahead, to see if it was safe enough on the streets, to get her into an air raid shelter. An air raid shelter being safer than a hotel. Otherwise, the hotel would have to do, somehow or other.

He raced down the corridor, whilst she tried to compose herself, straightening her hair and smoothing down her uniform, her only purpose now was to help the stricken people in the streets. He had only been gone a few minutes before there was a flash followed by an enormous explosion, knocking her to the ground. She knew the hotel had been struck.

Dazedly she forced herself to her feet, freeing herself from the debris in the room, managing to get to the door; everywhere there was smoke and a strange silence. Looking up, she could see the stars and an enormous gap, where the staircase used to be. There was still a banister to cling to, with part of the staircase still standing, she somehow managed to get to the ground. The hall was in a terrible state.

Susan felt her eyes smarting she tried to get accustomed to the dust and smoke assailing her. She heard a voice calling from the rubble, she knew it was his voice, desperately she hauled plaster, wood, marble away, with little effect. She was afraid at what to expect, she was shaking, from head to foot, she would have fallen, if a cheerful fireman had not caught her.

Before long the whole place came alive with A.R.P. Police, ambulances, doctors, all from nowhere. The fireman was shouting, 'Bring all the pumps you've got, the whole bloody world's on fire.'

Between them, they soon managed to get out the injured including Peter, and the dying. She accompanied him to the hospital, sitting down on the small bunk in the ambulance, her hands covering her face, terrified he would die. She knew that somehow she would have to pull herself together, and as soon as they reached the hospital, she attended to him, as well as other casualties. Going about her duties, as is the nature of a fully qualified nurse; giving first aid to the bleeding and dealing with first degree burns.

The doctor informed her that there was little hope for Peter, inasmuch he had multiple injuries. He was placed in the intensive care ward along with the dying.

She is demented. He is calling for her, but although she wants to stay with him, she has work to do, and somehow it gives her strength, to get through that terrible night. The hospital personnel are grateful and glad of her quiet efficiency. In the hospital there is a complete state of chaos, as the nearby mains have been blown by a high explosive, the windows are all shattered. There is no hot water, nothing seems to be working and the casualties seem to be pouring in from all sides, lining the corridors, the wards are overflowing. The lights have gone, and doctors and nurses are trying to cope with guttering candles and hurricane lamps. Operations are being carried out with the aid of generators on the most urgent cases, with blood everywhere, spurting out like fountains.

Some of the casualties lie dazed and in a state of shock. Others barely conscious, crying and hysterical. A nearby air raid shelter had been blown, and people are being carried into the Hospital in an unbelievable state. A woman who had been knitting was admitted with the knitting needles stuck in her abdomen. A man holding his pipe in his hand had been killed, still with the pipe in his hand. One by one the casualties are sorted out, the wards are cleared before noon the following day, enabling most casualties to be sent to Hospitals in the Home Counties, leaving the Hospitals in London free for further reception of casualties.

As the bombing of London raged, mothers were calling out to their children, and the children were calling out for their mothers, but they were not identified, and therefore, it was impossible to tell which child belonged to which mother. As the mothers lay dying they could hear their children in the distance calling for them, but the nurses were unable to let the mothers know that their children were safe at the end of the ward, because of non identification. There was no milk to feed the babies, which caused further problems.

In the beginning, during a heavy raid in London, the casualties were unimaginable, they were everywhere; the Hospitals were not prepared for such devastation, the smell of burning, smouldering, smoke and dust.

The nurses' faces were black, as they continued their gruesome work. If any glass was left in the windows, another thud and the glass was blown again. The casualties that were conscious sat up and screamed in their beds.

When dawn was breaking and Peter had died, Susan had the burden of having to tell other families that their relatives had also died in the night. She had the added sadness of having to control her tears to help them in their bereavement. The eyes of the firemen were being treated for burns, as she left the hospital in tears.

The sun began to break out on the beleaguered city. The fires were now abating, as the sirens blared out the all clear; splintered glass was being shovelled into the gutter by the indomitable cockneys; a haze blotted out the sun, as Susan slowly wended her way to Trafalgar Square.

She sat on the balustrade of the fountain, her small frame shaking with uncontrollable sobs…'Forty four years have gone by,' said Susan to herself, 'I can hardly believe it. Did it ever happen?'

Susan felt the tears fall down her face, as she remembered the events all those years ago. It seems like yesterday she thought to herself. She shivered in the cold November air of 1984, the sun had all but disappeared. She gathered her small belongings together and trundled down Whitehall to the Embankment. She walked along, passing Cleopatra's needle and leant against the balustrade staring into the lapping water. Was it her imagination, but there standing beside her was a very dark, beautiful girl, handsome in the Jewish way, with dark skin and large sad eyes?

'It was my fault,' said Susan bitterly, 'I should have been more responsible. I should not have let you out of my sight, and when I found you gone, I should have reported the fact, immediately.'

'It was not your fault,' said Rachel gently, putting her arm round the old lady's shoulder. 'It was our fault for not seeing the danger, before it was too late. It was my fault for only thinking of myself, and endangering the others, but most of all, it was my fault for being born a Jew.'

Chapter Six

Rachel's Story

Crowded round the board at the Clearing station were Sisters eager to find their names for the posting abroad; amongst the girls, Rachel was drawn to two of the Sisters. She smiled shyly at them, and they responded with like smiles. They introduced themselves as Susan Jones and Teresa O'Conner. Rachel Gelkop was tall, dark and graceful, with an olive skin and ethereal hazel eyes. Very reserved, she never allowed anyone to get too near her, and needed a lot of understanding. She was sensitive, dedicated, and an excellent nurse.

Every now and then, she would turn her eyes from the world, as if she were no longer there. Possibly her Jewish background made her deeper, more introspective than most people. She followed the Jewish religion strictly and devoutly, obeying it to the letter.

Rachel immediately liked the bubbling friendliness of Susan Jones, at the same time admiring the serene beauty of Teresa. She would look beautiful even in a sack, she thought, but her inward shyness made her reserved and seemingly unfriendly. She longed to be like them, and hoped her Jewish background would not be noticed, by either of them.

For the first fortnight, she gave lectures, teaching the Territorials how to save lives, their own and others. She also attended lectures herself. When she was lecturing, she came into her own, her eyes would brighten, and her whole demeanour would come alive. But, strangely, when she was with the other Sisters, she built a protective wall around herself, finding it difficult to talk about the ordinary things of life. Subjects which had been taken for granted by the others, the more fortunate than herself, or so she thought, it was easy for them; but, when a person such as she, had to struggle from the very beginning, then the outlook was very different. So, she became more silent and more introspective, apologetic for her own mistakes, and even others.

Rachel embarked in France, with her two friends, Susan and Teresa on March 10th 1940 with a contingent of others, headed by Matron marching onto a cross channel ferry, cheered on by the whistling troops. They were dressed in Army garb, tin hatted and rolled groundsheets on their backs. The day is dark and windy. As they left the shores of England and chugged away into the Channel, the ferry gave an almighty lurch, dipping down, and then up, like being on an everlasting swing.

The next days were chronic, as they swung unceremoniously in their hammocks at night, and clung onto ropes and railings during the day. Minefields had to be avoided at all costs, so the route took considerably longer. Rachel was not a good sailor. Most of the time, she felt queasy and sick, but her new good friends helped her on deck, finding some brandy which stopped her from vomiting. With their help, she managed to live on dry biscuits throughout a journey which should have taken only a few hours, but lasted three long days.

At last, they disembarked on launches sent from the shore. The neat ensemble was not quite so neat, as they clung to the side of the launches, with Matron staring stoically ahead. The boats skimmed through the waves, landing with flat smacks as they hit the roll of each wave and rushed to the shore. The nurses scrambled out on the quayside, looking green and shaken. Matron stepped ahead, like a hen with her rather tawdry chickens, looking neither to right or left, but to the awaiting trucks, well covered with red crosses at Cherbourg.

From Cherbourg they were taken through Caen, Rouen, Amiens, to Abbeville. On their way, the nurses were cheered by village folk, who put their thumbs up, waved, threw flowers and kisses to them, as they passed.

Eventually they arrived at the British Military Hospital, Abbeville (The 11th Casualty Clearing Station) to be led to their living quarters by Stacey Scott.

Rachel was secretly glad she was left to her freedom in a single room. She glanced at the furniture, and in her mind's eye, changed the dressing table to an Altar. Turning out her luggage, she put on the small chest of drawers, silver candlesticks for the Sabbath lights, a cup for the Sabbath bread to be sanctified. Having achieved careful unpacking, she looked at herself in the mirror, put a clean crisp uniform on with a white head veil, put scissors, fountain pen, and a handful of safety pins into her breast pocket, and left her room, acclimatising herself to the many corridors of this unusual hospital.

She familiarised herself with the ward she was working in, and was delighted to find herself working along with her friend Susan Jones. A course of plastic surgery, skin grafting, had been offered to them, and both nurses accepted gratefully, glad to be working usefully, at something other than the normal ward routine. How were they to know that the course would be cut after eight weeks, that the wards would be filled to overflowing by the casualties of Hitler's 'Blitzkrieg' and then to be hastily evacuated. So, they only learnt by theory, never by performance.

Just before sundown, on the Friday of her first week in the hospital, Rachel secretly went to her room, and carefully lit the candles in their silver containers; she took off her nurse's cap, and standing in the middle of the room, she spread out her hands between her eyes and the candles, she recited the prayer of ages gone. 'God, our God, King of the universe, who has sanctified us by your commandments, and commanded us to kindle the Sabbath lights.' A Christian prays to God, for God to help him to a better understanding of God; a Jew prays to God, so that he can work on himself, for the sake of God, therefore to a Jew, prayer is work, which must never become casual, and this is exactly what she wished to do, to work at all her religious duties.

The little room faded, and became a temple; she raised the beaker of wine in sanctification, the language seemed exalted; she is, after all, she told herself, one of God's chosen people. The high manner and style may be bizarre to the outsider, but to millions of homes, throughout the world, these words were being recited. There is a hymn which is close to the heart of most Jews, it can be sung, virtually to any tune, and with her eyes closed, she gently swayed from side to side, as the song gathered power, and transcended to the ceiling and beyond. It had a strange sensuous sweetness, an Arabic Spanish quality that overpowers the listener, and sends the singer into a trance, so that when the other nurses knocked on her door, Rachel was oblivious to them, and as the knocks grew louder and more persistent, they fell on deaf ears; she was not in this world.

Eventually, the door was swept open by Matron, followed by a bunch of giggling nurses, curious to see what was happening. Matron entered and stopped short, gaping at the transfixed nurse, she opened her mouth with a gasp and shut it again. The song stopped its flow in mid air, and slowly Rachel became aware of the people around her. She was angry with herself, and them. She, because she had become so imbued with the beauty of her religion, that she had forgotten that there was a realistic world she had to live in; and with them, bursting in on her privacy, for destroying her Sabbath.

'What is all this,' squawked Matron, gesticulating vaguely at the candles.

Rachel, with great dignity, gently blew the candles out, and with a trembling voice she turned to Matron. 'Unless a life is at stake, I will not be working on any Saturday, which is our Sabbath, from now on.' With that she pushed her way through the curious nurses at the door, and strode firmly out of the room.

'Well,' Matron echoed, following her out, surrounded by the cheerful ensemble of bright cheeked nurses.

'We've got a Yid amongst us,' they giggled, 'She's a Jew.'

Rachel applied to her task with added determination. Because of her background, she felt the others were wary of her, and therefore, she was anxious to be an outstanding nurse. She forced her own pace mercilessly, not only did she expect it from herself, she expected it from others, working with her. She was up at six thirty a.m. before the sleepy staff had gathered their senses, she would do her rounds, of bedpans, diets, breakfasts, temperatures etc; at eleven a.m. she took her place in classes for skin grafting, which entailed an eight month course of post operative management, as part of the course for plastic surgery.

From 10th May, however, her classes were cut short. Casualties began to fill the wards. Men were being brought in every day, with horrific skin burns, open wounds, gangrene, insidiously gaining control in leg and arms.

Although classes were cancelled, she gained practical experience by action, rather than text book knowledge. The Sisters would cut away uniforms, reeking with blood, clean the wound, then, stand by, while the surgeons took over the operations; whilst operating on gaping wounds, the surgeons kept to their teaching routines, but, instead of learning on dummies, or each other, the nurses were given the real thing, living supplies. Rachel watched fascinated, as she gathered into the operating theatre, where lay a badly wounded soldier with an open wound torn into his thigh by shrapnel.

Mr Williams, the bearded surgeon, took a skin grafting knife, cut quickly and decisively into a convenient donor site, transferring the partial thickness skin to re-surface the open wound. He then turned to the Sisters, and said, 'You then dress the wound with anti bacterial substances,' he looked round at the eager faces, 'Pinch graft with your scalpel or needle, implant further skin round the edges, rather like bed planting, and put a dressing over them, you will find the donor site will heal itself.' With these words, he left the nurses to bandage, and make the patient as comfortable as possible, to be returned to the ward. He never stopped his grim and gruesome task, supported by his team, and the ever willing nurses.

Rachel would crawl into her bed at night, utterly exhausted, knowing full well she still had to write long copious notes of what she had learnt in the day. Many times, though, her exhaustion, would overcome her, her eyelids would droop, she would fall asleep, with her pencil still in her hands. Next morning, she was back again, 6.30 a.m. doing her rounds. 'I will be the best amongst them, they will find that they cannot do without me, I will be indispensable,' she vowed firmly to herself.

As the morning wore on, Rachel came across her friend Teresa, trying to listen to Churchill's speech over a battered radio, with his own peculiar form of invective, delivered in his own distinctive delivery.

'The British and French have advanced to rescue not only Europe, but mankind, from the foulest and most soul destroying tyranny, that has ever darkened and stained the pages of history.' The radio spluttered and became indistinct.

'If I saw a German coming down that path,' said Teresa, glancing quickly out of the window, 'I would scream and faint.'

'That's a lot of good,' said Rachel, as they both relieved the two weary night Sisters, little knowing that only a few kilometres away a small British Force was trying to hold Louvain.

The ward was filling with casualties. The French were in disarray, retreating fast against the invincible German Army. The surgeons saw little of the days, but the wards quickly coped with the wounded, mainly for shock treatment; the stretcher bearers came again and again, until there was literally no room to put a foot between the stretchers. The men were in a pitiable condition, past meaningful speech and communication.

Rachel and Teresa never stopped. Uniforms had to be cut off, caked with blood, boots sliced with razors, blood pressures taken, wounds redressed. Everything Rachel had learnt came to her rescue after four years of tough training. Her experience of the running lecture, given only yesterday by the surgeon Mr Williams, gave her hands a sure and steady skill, as she replaced dressings over gaping wounds, at the same time, administered morphia injections.

She learned too, of the enormous benefits of sulphonamide drugs, the Blood Transfusion Service and penicillin being introduced therapeutically. She had seen that early surgery, inoculations all helped to contain the casualty rate, although the wounded were packed so tightly, there was hardly room for the nurses to move.

Mainly, they were given intensive treatment for shock, until they were sufficiently restored to undergo surgery, they would then be returned to the wards.

The days fell into night, with searchlights sweeping the skies, and distant flashes glimmered in the darkness. A lot of times the tired nurses would practically sleep where they stood, falling into bed in a stupor. Up again at seven a.m., the whole roundabout would be repeated.

This particular day, as Rachel went into the ward, she fancied her name was called. She looked down, and noticed that two men had been brought in during the night. One of them, his eyes closed, was obviously swinging between reality and consciousness. He had a leg wound, which had turned gangrenous. This was the problem. He would be passed back from the front line, to one dressing station after another, until he arrived at the hospital, sometimes ten miles away from where he had been wounded. He opened his eyes again, and whispered, 'Am I dying, nurse?'

Rachel bent down and replied, 'No, don't worry,' and she took his hand and pressed it. A slight smile passed his lips as he lapsed into unconsciousness again. Rachel was left with Teresa to carry out resuscitation. Gently she cradled him, whilst Teresa soaped and sponged his back. They eased on clean pyjamas, cleansed his furred tongue and crusted lips, gave him an injection of morphia, and left him to sleep.

As the day wore on, their usual neat appearance became more and more dishevelled.

'Before I go off duty,' said Rachel, 'I'll see how our two new patients are getting on.'

'Your boyfriend is awake,' said Teresa, 'and calling your name.'

Rachel went over to the bed and whispered in his ear, 'How are you feeling?'

His eyes flickered open and he said, 'All the better for seeing you.'

Rachel decided to stay with him throughout the night. His head turned from side to side which denoted inward haemorrhage, and he stared unseeingly round the room. Every now and then his eyes fixed on her face, dark staring eyes. She did not tell him, she had been informed that his leg would have to be amputated. From time to time she checked his blood pressure, moistened his dry lips, she often held his hand, it seemed to bring him comfort.

He was a young man, brown complexioned with dark curly hair, and deep luminous eyes. He could have come from the Middle East, of Arab or Moorish background. There was something attractive about him, and his very vulnerability, lying there, appealed to her. Rachel was determined to get him well, and used all her nursing skills to help him.

The next day, as Rachel went about her morning rounds, she worked thoroughly, keeping her thoughts, as well as she could, away from where he lay. His bed was enclosed by curtains, the operation was taking place she was told, and the leg would be amputated. After a while, she was relieved to see him back in the ward, although his face was whiter than the pillows he lay on. The technique of the stump bandage, learnt in training school, was commonplace here, amongst so many amputations. The medical C.O. went from bed to bed in his round of patients, keeping up a running commentary, 'Quarter of morphia here, straight away, two pints of blood there…'

Rachel went over to her favourite patient. His eyes were still closed, but, now there was a little more colour in his cheeks. 'How are you this evening Joseph?' She had heard of his name. He did not answer. She took his hand, 'Trust me,' she said, 'We will get you well.'

Next day, coming into the ward, she was delighted to see that all her care had come to some fruition. His eyes followed her wherever she went and she could see the gratitude in his face.

He looked forward to her coming to see him. She found that he was of French Moroccan background, and he would tell her, in his attractive accent, his life in Algeria. They had so much in common. He had been brought up in community life, in the Kibbutz, he talked about his strict religious training, as a boy into man.

Joseph had been caught up in the web of war, had been hastily conscripted into the French army, originally to defend the Maginot line, against the oncoming Germans. This defence was quickly swept aside by the enemy, and the French retreated, until they found the Germans had advanced on them, to such an extent, they had the miserable experience of having to turn about and follow the Germans, attacking them in the rear.

Several men of his regiment had absconded altogether. He also informed her proudly, that when the war was over, he had hopes of becoming a Rabbi. Emotionally, he grasped her hand, 'Will you help me? With you by my side I can conquer the world,' he laughed, and then added more seriously, 'Rachel, I want you, I want you physically, spiritually, I want you to be my wife.'

Rachel was overcome by this unexpected outburst, 'Don't you think we should wait until the war is over?' she compromised.

'No,' he said.

She could see he was used to getting his own way. 'But,' she faltered 'Matron will never allow it.'

'Leave Matron to me,' he said firmly. Rachel was confused, she could not understand her emotions. In the normal way, she would have gently evaded this kind of advance, realising the boys were far from home, away from mothers, and sweethearts. They were also in a very weakened condition. Why was she so overwhelmed by this sweet stranger? Somehow, she felt it had to be, she did not want to resist this soft sensual excitement that swept over her like a tide.

She spent all her time with him. In those days, patients were kept in bed for weeks, before being allowed up to face the world. Each night, he excitedly made his plans for marriage. He told her, he had volunteered to join the Army. He had a smattering of languages, particularly German. He knew his scriptures backwards, and he had his own version of Bible stories, full of humour and

Jewish wisecracks, but, even so, still faithfully told. His knowledge of life, for such a young man, was immense. There was some urgency about their relationship, which left her breathless.

Rachel whispered to him, 'I have no wedding dress,' this did not deter him. 'The arms must be covered and a veil over the head, this must be observed.'

Joseph and Rachel agreed between them, that she would stay working at the hospital after they were married, until he managed to get his discharge from the Army. In the meantime they would snatch as much happiness as they could.

Rachel found herself obtaining a certificate from the Superintendent Registrar for marriages of the District permitting marriages by certificate or licence. Next she went to the local Synagogue, although, in this case, the bridegroom was not a member of the Synagogue, but the Rabbi bypassed this rule when he heard from Rachel her reasons for this marriage, and how very ill her fiancé still happened to be, and only just recovering from his severe wounds. The Rabbi was only too pleased to be prepared to officiate at her wedding, and he agreed to marry them at the hospital. All antagonism between Rachel and the other nurses faded away over her love affair. They were delighted for her, and kept her secret well hidden from Matron. The nurses went to work with a will on her marriage, determined to make it the most memorable day of her life.

Teresa found curtains belonging to the casino, and although covered with dust, she pulled them down, steamed them in the bathroom and gave them to Rachel for her wedding dress. The velvet was a beautiful shade of green, and with no further ado, they set to work with an old sewing machine which they found hidden in a corner, and within two or three days the dress was ready.

Matron was informed by Joseph of their forthcoming marriage, and with his charm and insistence, she soon succumbed, apart from a few grumbles about the dangers of wartime marriages. The great day was set for May 16th 1940.

Little did any of them realise, that the remnants of the British Expeditionary Force were fighting a desperate battle against the victorious Germans, only a few kilometres away, to save Louvain. They had no news for two days; the radio had packed in, some time ago. The growing army of refugees, deserting soldiers, pouring steadily past their gates, were the only signs that evacuation would soon be the order of the day.

All the nurses were determined to enjoy the forthcoming marriage. The day dawned bright and sunny, as were all these days before the wholesale destruction of the world. Both Rachel and Joseph fasted on their wedding day, as was normal for an Orthodox couple. They offered special prayers upon entering a new life, encouraged and fortified by the knowledge they do so with Divine Grace.

The nurses helped to dress Joseph's beautiful bride. Her dark hair, entwined with green and gold leaves, was covered with a cream veil. Her green velvet dress, they had laboriously made for her, fell to the floor in flowing folds, with long sleeves intricately covered with gold thread, also at the collar.

The Rabbi, whose name was also Gold, Rabbi Gold, arrived bringing with him a small portable gramophone. The hospital ward was filled with musical incantations of previous recorded marriages. He also brought with him the outstanding feature of Jewish weddings, the rectangular canopy of Chuppah, made of silk and velvet, supported upon four poles, about five or six feet apart. It symbolised the home to which the bridal couple are about to set up. This is held over the head of the bridegroom. All heads of the guests had to be covered, but as most of the guests were nurses, their heads were covered anyway, by tulle caps.

Rachel was brought in by the Medical Company Officer, who stood in for her father, and who gave her away. The men stood on the side of the bridegroom, the women beside the bride. The bridal party then stood under the Canopy with the officiating Minister in front of them. The marriage ceremony opened with a blessing of welcome from the Psalms pronounced by the Rabbi, followed by a Psalm of thanksgiving, and an address to the bridal pair. Following this, the Minister pronounces the betrothal blessing.

Joseph was raised in his bed with pillows. The Rabbi addressed both parties. 'You, Joseph Kahn and you, Rachel Gelkop, are about to be wedded according to the laws of Moses and Israel. Will you, Joseph Kahn, take this woman Rachel Gelkop, to be your wife? Will you be a true and faithful husband unto her? Will you protect and support her? Will you love, honour and cherish her?'

Joseph answered, 'I will.'

'Behold thou art consecrated unto me by this ring according to the law of Moses and Israel.' Rachel bent down beside her beloved Joseph. He placed a ring on the first finger of her right hand, and declared to his wife the central prayer of the Siddur service.

Long after the guests had departed and their future had been toasted in champagne bought by the nurses, Rachel stayed by the side of Joseph. This was their honeymoon, looking after him, seeing after his every wish and compelling him to get better. Of course, their marriage could not be consummated at this stage, as Joseph was still extremely ill, but Rachel was not concerned. She was ecstatically happy. Matron had given her permission to have a few days off duty, to be by his side.

But her happiness was short lived. Evacuation had been announced, and all nurses, wounded, medical personnel, went ahead to be transferred by ambulance to an awaiting train at Abbeville. But a handful of badly wounded would be left behind for further evacuation, in a day or two, when transportation would be easier. Amongst that handful was Joseph.

Rachel pleaded to stay with her husband, but Matron was adamant. Rachel would be badly needed to look after the first contingent of wounded, and she was to leave immediately, that was an order. She practically had to be torn away from him, weeping uncontrollably, but he reassured her that it would only be a day or two, before he was by her side again.

Rachel was ordered onto the last truck of the convoy, with Susan Jones, Stacey Scott and Teresa O'Conner, along with medical personnel in ambulances.

Rachel jumped down from the truck at Abbeville station. Although her thoughts were only of Joseph, they were abruptly interrupted by Stacey, 'Rachel, for heaven's sake, wake up, and follow me.' She saw Stacey had in tow three undernourished children. 'Go over to that Gendarme, and tell him to open those food shops in the station, you can speak French fluently. Tell him, that is an order.'

Rachel obeyed swiftly, it was folly to disobey Stacey in one of her moods. She pushed through the crowds, and spoke to the policeman to open the shops, but she was refused point blank. 'No, no, the owners will be back, and I will lose my job,' even gentle persuasion had no effect. She could see he was at the end of his tether, he could not cope with the crowd.

But, Stacey was determined. 'Open the shop, at once,' she ordered. Eventually, after much voluble French, he agreed.

The door gave way under a cloud of dust, and Rachel, with a stream of mothers following her, entered the dim interior. Dispensing the tinned milk and food amongst the children was like the parable of the loaves and fishes, she thought, the feeding of the ten thousand. If only she could do the same, but before long, within a few minutes the shelves had been laid bare by the crowd. The three nurses had seen that the children were fed, because of the Gendarme, ordered by Stacey to keep back the crowd, in spite of further grumblings.

At that precise moment, when they were about to enter a further shop, again forcing the door, they all had to rush for cover. There is nothing quite like the terror of a three hundred mile an hour dive, even from a lone bomber. The plane roared as it dived terrifyingly, first the scream, then the pounding of bombs, as they struck the station and around. The crowd at the station fell over themselves, in their panic to avoid the bombs, leaving themselves open to the machine gun fire of the lone raider.

When the smoke cleared, bodies of innocent refugees lay on the ground. As the nurses emerged, shaken, black with dust and grime, Rachel said to the others, 'If Matron could see us now, she would have something to complain about.' With unsteady, tottering legs, they picked their way through the carnage of dead and dying to the station platform.

Incredulously, they stared at each other in disbelief, when they found their train had gone. They were devastated, and petrified; the obvious answer, as Stacey suggested, was to go back to the Hospital to provide help with the second plan of evacuating the few patients remaining.

Chapter Seven

Evacuation was to take place, so they understood, within a day or two. This was easier said than done. Before, they were in vehicles, going the same way as the refugees; now, they were forcing a passage back, through the oncoming crowd, but they found, if they kept to the side of the roads, they could slowly push their way back to the hospital. It seemed to Rachel so unreal. Behind them in the background lay the blazing town, but instead of feeling depressed and frightened, she was elated to find herself going back to being reunited with her husband. Fate had been good to her, she told herself. She was not meant to leave his side.

The road was protected each side by long graceful trees, yellow fields, yellow meadows, stretching away to woods and hills, the landscape was so peaceful. But, the peaceful scene lasted only for a short while. An aeroplane rapidly approached overhead, and the old familiar rat-a-tat-tat of the machine gun as it fired indiscriminately on the long line of refugees below.

Within seconds, the road cleared, as people rushed in panic to the ditches. Rachel stared at the plane, she could not move, as a rabbit with a cobra. Stacey hurled herself at her and threw her to the ground. The plane roared overhead, there was a terrifying pause, as if the world had stopped, then all pandemonium broke out. Women and children were screaming; the three nurses set to work with their first aid bags, but there was little they could do with their meagre equipment. Death swept through the crowd like a wave. The crowd rushed on, however, putting as many kilometres as they could between the Germans and themselves.

Rachel was amazed at their callousness. They saw her, trying to stop the blood from a bullet wound in a child's thigh on the wayside, and, at the same time, comforting the hapless mother. Anybody who stepped in the way of the crowd, either living or dead, were angrily thrust aside; there was no time for sentimentality for the bereaved; in fact, the crowd would turn on them, shouting furiously, 'Don't waste your time on the wounded.'

The three nurses, covered with blood, were just deciding to cut through the woods onto, hopefully, less congested roads, when a girl about the age of sixteen threw herself down on the verge of a ditch, screaming and shouting, there was no escape. 'The Germans were everywhere,' she screamed. 'Give yourselves up,' then she started hysterically laughing and crying. 'If you don't give in, we women will be raped and murdered.'

Rachel and Stacey ran over to her and tried to quieten her; the girl would not be quietened, she hit out at them, still screaming, 'It will be the worst for us, if you refuse to give in to them.' Stacey tried to cope with a tranquilliser injection. The girl was frightening the crowd, and there could be a stampede with children crushed underfoot.

At that moment, two French soldiers emerged from the crowd, and came over to the girl, whom the nurses had propped against a tree; one of them, roughly shaking her by the shoulder, 'Where do you come from? Your papers please.'

This time the girl tried to run away, making a dash for the woods, hitting out at those who held her. 'Let me go,' she screamed, still laughing and crying. 'The Germans will get you all.'

The soldiers seized her again, and again asked for her identification documents. She showed them documents from a small village in Alsace, they began to question her. It was well known that people from Alsace were pro German at that time, and before long she admitted her father was German. There was an uneasiness in her eyes now, she had already dropped her madness ploy. Under their fierce scrutiny, she was unable to say where she came from.

The nurses felt sorry for the girl, they considered she must have gone through terrible suffering which had affected her brain.

Without explanation, the soldiers dragged the girl to the nearby woods, the nurses watched them, stultified, they could do nothing. The soldiers took a long time, before they emerged, with grim expressions.

'Clear case of fifth column,' they said, casually, to the stunned nurses. 'These people are sent to start panic. We have had dozens of reports of the same nature, all over France.' They produced a notebook allegedly found in the girl's pocket, with details of her work, written in German. 'Shooting is too good for them.'

The nurses were speechless, and with these words, they pocketed the notebook, and strode away. The nurses looked at each other in consternation. A young girl had possibly been raped and shot before their eyes, on threadbare evidence. Meanwhile the crowd had become angry, venting their hostility on the Government that had abandoned them. People were collapsing on the roadside, through heat and lack of food and water. The nurses tried to obtain water to help the refugees from nearby farms, but everywhere they went they were refused, so, without further ado, they turned into the lanes and bypasses they knew so well, to reach the hospital.

As they approached the gates, they were surprised to find the place deserted. They had imagined they would have been inundated with refugees, but not one refugee was to be seen; they were too busy getting away from the Germans, they surmised. The hospital looked deserted. The nurses skirted round the hospital, looking through the windows, they then decided to try the doors.

Rachel called to the others excitedly, 'They are unlocked. Come on.'

'We look like blood stained scarecrows,' said Stacey aptly.

But, Rachel didn't hear her, she was only concerned at finding Joseph. She ran into the ward where they had all worked in, for so long, and without hesitation, she threw herself into the arms of her beloved husband. He looked happy and in good health, and was overjoyed at seeing her again. He had obviously been well looked after, by the few remaining staff left behind. Rachel was relieved to find him, able to care for himself, and to get about the ward with the aid of a crutch.

Laughing and crying, she told him what had befallen the three nurses at Abbeville station. 'We are all together now,' she said, looking round the ward at the few remaining patients, 'whatever happens, we will look after you, as well as we can. Who's brewing the tea?'

'I am,' said their dear friend Sergeant Major Thompson, thrusting a mug of tea into her hands. They all gathered round him, eager for any news from the Allied Forces.

'When are they coming to evacuate us?' was on everyone's lips.

His cheerfulness kept their spirits up, and helped them to come to grips with the situation, which could turn against them at any moment. They talked long into the night, and were instructed, if evacuation did not materialise, to defend themselves as well as possible. He then solemnly gave each nurse a pistol, and brief instructions on the use of them.

'I know it will not come to this,' he said, 'as we have every hope of being evacuated in the next few hours. But, it is our duty, in whatever country we happen to be in, to escape, to be free.'

Rachel took her pistol, holding it tentatively like a diseased rat, and brought it over to Joseph. 'I won't know what to do with this, you take it,' she said to Joseph who put it under his pillow. 'We will not need it, anyway,' she continued, 'we will be back in England before long, and this time, I will never leave you again.'

Dawn broke on this Tuesday, grey and sullen.

Although Rachel had been up practically all night, she was not tired, she went about her tasks as if nothing had happened, fussing around Joseph, correcting his posture against the pillows. She chatted to him, speaking happily of their future life together in England, where they would be safe; they would be evacuated today or tomorrow, and in no time they would be heading for the cliffs of Dover. Joseph lay quietly back watching her, as she fluttered round his bed, he was tentative and uneasy.

The other nurses were ready with stretchers, blood bottles, etc, for a quick evacuation. They waited all day with shadows lengthening in the wards. Unknown to them the Germans were advancing with uncanny speed. They entered a village long before they were expected, before the French could blow up the petrol pumps, so the Germans could automatically 'fill up' as they advanced.

On that same grey and sullen day May 21st, 1940, Amiens fell to the Germans at dawn, and by the afternoon the railway junction of Abbeville, on the Somme Estuary, was occupied by German cyclist troops.

Teresa went to the window and opened it, and stepped back with a gasp, turning white. Exactly as she had predicted, there, on the path beneath her was a German Officer, unperturbed, smoking a cigarette, trying to enter at the main entrance. As soon as he found the entrance blocked, he shouted at his soldiers, who, with their machine-guns, blasted the lock on the door.

They were all under the impression that the hospital was empty. The officer was issuing instructions to his subalterns, and humming as he came up the steps of the main entrance to the hallway. They were laughing and joking, as they kicked each door open; they were still not taking any chances, however. After satisfying themselves that there was no one in the building, so they thought, they turned their attention to the marble stairs. The Officer sped up the stairs swiftly, and repeated the same actions, as they cautiously kicked open the doors of each ward.

The two men, Sergeant Major Thompson and the Medical Orderly, stationed themselves behind the door of the ward with the five patients, including Joseph. The nurses hid themselves behind anything affording shelter. They could hear heavy boots against polished floors, as the Germans passed through the empty wards. Then the boots stopped outside their door, the order was issued, a burst of gunfire, and with a kick the door was thrown open. The officer could only have been about twenty four years old, and the look of surprise as he fell under a hail of bullets would be imprinted on her mind forever, Rachel thought. Then in swift succession the alerted Germans, with machine guns blazing, blasted their way into the ward. The orderly was swiftly dealt with, but the trained Sergeant Major Thompson was a different proposition. The first soldier was gunned down and lay on the floor in a pool of blood, shrieking for his 'mutter'.

In the interchange of bullets, Joseph was caught in a midstream volley and was killed instantly. Rachel dashed to him, and sank to her knees, screaming and clutching his bedclothes, involuntarily, in her agony. For one second Thompson turned towards her, and this action was to cost him his life; for in that split second his body was sprayed with bullets by the second soldier. He slumped by the door, dropping his gun which sped over the polished floor within the grasp of Rachel. The soldier turned his gun towards Rachel, but the gun jammed.

'Kill the bastard' shouted Stacey, but Rachel was beyond doing anything, 'I can't. I can't kill,' she moaned. Stacey made a dash for the gun at the same time as the soldier, but a well aimed knee between the legs left the man immobilised. She grabbed the gun and with a burst of fire killed him. Stacey did not dare to stop or look round, she threw herself through the window, relaxing her body as she did so, and landed on the flower beds beneath. The shock knocked the breath from her body, but she scrambled up and ran as fast as she could. Rachel was out of her mind with grief, pathetically trying to revive her dead husband.

When the Gestapo came on the scene, they found a distraught nurse praying beside the body, and although they thought she was incanting prayers, in her frenzy, she was reciting, over and over again, part of the Hippocratic oath. 'I invoke all the Gods to be my witnesses,' as if she had to cleanse herself of her tremendous guilt. 'Whatever house I enter, there will I go for the benefit of the sick, refraining from wrong doing and corruption.' In between these outbursts, she begged forgiveness for her weakness of not defending him. She blamed herself for his death.

Brutally they dragged her away from his bedside, but she turned on them, clawing and spitting. She no longer cared what they did to her. She was lucky they did not kill her on the spot. The leader of the group, seemingly known as Kapetyn, with his narrow eyes, gaunt face, stared suspiciously round the ward, 'How many Jews are patients here?' and with a sign to his second-in-command, 'Get rid of them,' he said briefly.

The other proceeded systematically to put a bullet through the heads of the five remaining patients. They were too weak to resist, then turning to Rachel, he said, 'Have you been nursing these Jews? Are you a Jew lover?' He put his face close to hers, searching fixedly into her eyes. Without turning away, he rasped, 'Papers?'

With trembling hands, she turned out her top pocket, where an accumulation of safety pins, buttons and a thermometer, dropped and smashed on the floor. She handed over her identification papers.

He alighted on her name. 'Gelkop' he muttered, 'Gelkop that is not an English name, that is a Jewish name from Poland or the Ukraine, or somewhere.' He continued staring at her papers. Kapetyn was so intent on identifying Rachel as a Jewess that he did not search the ward, and did not notice Teresa doubled up, under the bed of one of the dead patients. Teresa was petrified, with her hands in her ears, and her eyes tightly shut. The Germans were only intent on their Jewish captive.

The second-in-command to Kapetyn shoved Rachel out of the ward, and against the corridor wall. Kapetyn ordered her to empty the rest of her pockets, and take off her rings and pocket watch. Rachel hesitated, taking off her newly acquired wedding ring.

'Not fast enough, Jew,' Kapetyn struck her hard across the face, and pushed her down the balustrade steps in front of him. Rachel, her legs buckling, brushed the blood off her lips with her hand, a bruise darkening on the side of her face. She steadied herself, but every time a tremendous shove from behind nearly knocked her down, and she saw the hospital entrance as a blur. There must be someone she could complain to, someone with integrity, who would discipline these men, some senior officer, she thought.

They sat beside her, in the limousine that sped quickly through the streets. Where were they taking her? Back through the town of Abbeville. The town was a pall of smoke, with some of the houses still spluttering fire, others empty shells, rising starkly against the sky. One of the men spoke to the driver, who, after speeding through many streets, drew up outside the local Synagogue of fifteenth century origin. Rachel recognised it instantly as the Synagogue she had previously attended, to acquire the blessing of a Rabbi, for her wedding at the hospital. Kapetyn was the first to get out of the car.

'Get out,' he ordered Rachel. The others dragged out the helpless nurse. Kapetyn ran up the steps to the Synagogue, shouting over his shoulder, to his driver and second-in-command to collect as many Jews as they could find from the neighbouring streets and houses, and order them to proceed immediately to the Synagogue. At the same time a small detachment of the SS or Special Duty Groups, set up machine-guns along the route and surroundings of the Synagogue.

The Jews were lined in an orderly queue and marched into the Synagogue and Rachel was thrust into line with them. Jewellery, necklaces, and rings were snatched off necks and fingers, before they passed through the doors. At that time, the Jews had not recognised their danger. Abbeville had only just fallen to the Germans, and after all, life had to go on, sanity would surely re-assert itself after a few months, and peace once again would take the upper hand, or so they thought.

The scene to Rachel as she was pushed into the Synagogue was unforgettable. In the dim light, she could perceive the congregation of Orthodox Jews, beards, sidelocks, and prayer shawls being lined up in front of her, but, unbelievably she saw shuffling along in the same line, was the Rabbi Gold who married her. It was stifling hot, as more and more people pressed through the narrow opening. On a table in front of the Ark was the Talmud. A crisp authoritative voice crackled through the tannoy, ordering each person to pull out a page from the Talmud, and tear it into little pieces, then stamp on it, grinding it into the floor with their heel. The profanity of such an action overcame her; to be forced into such overwhelming irreverence and to desecrate the religion she had held most dear, was abhorrent to her.

There was no shamming, no half measures. Surely the Rabbi, in front of her, would refuse, would stand up against these bullies, and decry them for what they were, but no, he hesitated for a moment, then with his hand, he pulled out a page, tore it into little pieces and trod it into the ground, and without a backward glance, he passed on.

Rachel did the same. Her hand shook, as she pulled out a page, rent it into tiny shreds, and crushed it under her foot; as she did so she murmured 'God forgive me.'

Kapetyn whirled round, his eyes like black coals in his pale face. 'There is no God here,' he screamed at her, 'God will not save you now.'

With the butts of their guns, the soldiers pushed her back through the entrance of the Synagogue to the waiting car. Why had he chosen her, and maybe saved her life?

Kapetyn shouted further commands to the soldiers, their guns trained on the Synagogue as he stepped into the car. They were deliberately setting it alight. When the people tried to escape, they were caught in the machine-gun fire. Rachel hid her face in her hands, she could not believe what she had been forced to do and witness. Through her stupidity and cowardice, she had not only lost her husband, but she had turned against God and sinned against Him.

Kapetyn dragged her hands from her face. 'Where is your God now?' he whispered, his face close to hers.

Chapter Eight

Rachel could smell the alcoholic vapour on his breath, the rancid smell of rye from whisky intake, and she recoiled from him in horror. 'I believe in God,' she whispered.

Kapetyn was seeking redemption from the private misery in his heart. He looked gloomily out of the window. 'Why doesn't He help you, then? Why doesn't He help his chosen people?' he added sarcastically. 'Why? Because He does not exist.'

'He works in mysterious ways,' she blurted out. Drunkenly he forced her hands down from her face, but the intensity of his eyes was dangerous. 'These Jews are destroying us,' he said. 'The more we kill them, the more they are there. I can't sleep because of them, when I wake up, they are still there staring at me.' He put his hand up, as if to ward off invisible people. 'We rid the world of them, but still they come back.'

His next words struck terror in her heart, 'Where you are going, my dear, do not waste your time praying.' Kapetyn then turned away from her, as if she no longer existed, issued a further order to the driver, and sat back in silence. He had lost all interest in her, and having overcome his conscience in alcohol, he felt no sense of sin from the butchery he had just been party to; and with the absence of sin, the absence of God was inseparable.

The car stopped outside the police station in Abbeville, which had recently been taken over by the Gestapo. Rachel was marched into a large room at the end of which sat the interrogator, at a typewriter. There was a long queue of prisoners, as she approached the desk.

The interrogator barked at her, 'Name, address, occupation?' She answered as well as she could. 'Married?'

'Yes.'

'Jewish?' She hesitated.

Kapetyn who stood beside the interrogator, spoke for her. 'Yes,' he stated firmly.

She was handed a yellow star that had to be sewn on her uniform, immediately.

'Noses to the wall,' was the next order. She was shoved towards the wall by the rifles of the soldiers. A door opened, 'Women prisoners, queue up and follow me.' The thick legged woman led them to another desk, each woman gave her name, and placed on the desk, jewellery, wallets, and French francs. In front of Rachel was a small stout woman who clung to her rings and refused to part with them. 'They are mine,' she shouted, 'my husband gave them to me.'

What good were her rings to her now, thought Rachel; what madness possessed this woman? Didn't she understand what they would do to her?

The soldiers intervened. 'Spread your hands on the desk,' they commanded, and although she sobbed and cried throughout, each ring was unceremoniously and roughly taken from her fingers.

Rachel placed her little purse, the red one, given to her by Joseph, and emptied it in front of the thick-legged woman. The procession of women pressed down the corridor, which was lined on each side with cells. Another woman, in uniform, was fitting a large key into the metal doors, and all prisoners were dispatched into them, an endless world of prison doors. Rachel's cell was dark and narrow, with a rolled straw pallet at the end, on a wooden planked bed. In the corner a small latrine. The door banged behind her, and she heard the key turn in the lock. Alone, the light snapped off in the middle of the room. She sat huddled on the stinking straw pallet still in her uniform and grateful for the warmth of her nurse's cloak, which she wrapped tightly round her. She imagined she must be in the town's penitentiary. It was bitterly cold and damp. What had she done, to bring down all the wrath of these people? Her mind confusedly tried to piece together all that had transpired, in the last few days; she was numb from grief and shock.

If they killed her, which was a possibility, what had she to lose anyway? Yet she was frightened of death, there was something defeatist about death. She told herself to be mature and practical and to fight back, seemingly subjective to them, but, to use all her cunning to survive, and with that last thought she fell asleep.

The next thing she knew, it was morning. A tiny plate had been pushed through a slit in the cell door, a watery substance of gruel and a hunk of bread. The door was reopened and a grim faced guard marched her out to the shower room. The joy of the water raining down on her bruised eye and matted hair. Rachel was amongst many women, and they jumped about like spring lambs, laughing, kicking, splashing about in their new found freedom, if only momentarily. Soap was abundant, and they used it liberally.

Some of the prisoners had been here for months, even years, and had lived in the same garments since they were arrested. Rachel was able to ascertain various stories through her knowledge of languages, and she considered herself lucky, having only been in prison for a few days. Her blood stained uniform was handed back to her, which she quickly donned, with her cloak.

'Prisoners will follow me,' the same grim faced female guard marched them back to their cells. In her cell, high up, was a window. If she climbed onto her bed, she could see the tops of swaying trees, and the blue sky, and catch the sun on her face. This small happiness she looked forward to everyday, when the sun woke her in the morning, and stayed for a few hours. With a little effort, prising herself onto her toes, she could see even further, the barbed wire surrounding the prison, and the forests beyond.

Rachel had no idea how long she had been in this prison, the days seemed endless, and the nights longer. She could speak perfect German, like most Jews, through her knowledge of Hebrew. One day, the Guards shouted through every cell, 'Collect all possessions in pillow cases' was the order. 'All prisoners are to be deported.'

'Deported, but where?' Rachel was in a fever of excitement, she was to leave this prison at last. With trembling hands, she dropped the few articles belonging to her, her crumpled uniform, her cap, brush, which was wrapped in her cap into the pillow case. She had been given a faded cotton dress, and threadbare coat with the hem down on one side. She was considerably thinner, but she still brushed her hair vigorously every day, and although she had no make-up, her beauty was unmatched, with her large dark eyes, thick hair, and olive skin. She stood at her cell door, clutching her pillow case. Then came further orders and clanging of prison doors. She stepped into the hall, and was led along a corridor, into a courtyard, where a row of machine-guns had been set up. There was a thick layer of sawdust on the ground.

'Get to the wall, face it.'

So this was to be her destination, she thought, and tried to prepare herself for the end. She lined up with the other women, some were sobbing and praying 'Tiskaddal veyiskaddash'. The words flowed like tears. There was a burst of firing. The Germans roared with laughter. A man was strutting up and down behind them.

'Jews, those who cheat the German Reich will be shot,' he shouted, 'Those who try to escape will be shot.' His voice became conciliatory, even persuasive, 'We do everything for your own good, we will protect you, as long as you obey us, in everything we ask, we will look after you. It is up to you. Form five ranks.'

Some of the women fainted, they were left where they were lying. They all shuffled into ranks.

At the end of each rank sat an S.S. Officer with papers of each individual in front of him. He looked up at Rachel, 'Name?' he enquired.

'Rachel Gelkop' she answered. She saw on his desk a small photograph of herself, her identification and particulars were beside the photograph. He took up a large rubber stamp and banged it down across her face 'To be deported. Destination Unknown.'

With rifle butts in their backs, they were pushed into grey buses, the windows of which were painted over. The bus was so overcrowded they could not possibly fall, they were packed in like sardines.

'Where are we going?' they whispered amongst themselves. The answer seemed to be a transit camp near Paris, and then on to a work camp called Lublin, in Poland. Where were all her friends, and her husband? All dead, it would have been better if they had killed her as well, she thought. The buses screeched to a halt.

The guards were tense and shrill. 'Form ranks' they shrieked.

The old and ill were beaten mercilessly, as they tried to shuffle into some semblance of order. When they emerged from the buses, they found themselves in a railway siding, beside a long row of unlit railway coaches, the windows of which had been painted and barred.

Cattle wagons were waiting there, eighty people to a wagon. A few loaves of bread and buckets of water. Then the cars were sealed, a prolonged whistle, the wheels began to grind, and Rachel along with the rest was on her way. Destination unknown.

On the fourth day, the train stopped at Lublin railway station. The doors opened and spewed out hundreds of miserable, bedraggled people. They were greeted with a military march, which had a lot to do with restoring their spirits. Perhaps it was not so bad, as they had imagined. They quite cheerfully marched in time with the music to a reception committee, where they were counted by guards holding whips, accompanied by dogs. Every morning at four thirty a.m. Rachel was forced to stand, with rows of suffering inmates for roll calls, lasting two hours, at least. Then, they were forced to march, again to a lively military band, to work, felling trees, potato picking, heaving coal until seven at night. Midmorning they were given a half hour break for a bowl of cabbage soup. At night, they were issued with a piece of bread, lump of cheese, or sausage. Cabbage and carrot soup in summer, a mixture of oats and water in the winter. Rachel had lost all sense of time. It seemed to her, this miserable existence would last for ever. The months rolled by. February was a bitter month in 1942. Whirlpools of snow were driven in all directions by a harsh east wind.

To understand the relationship between Hans Horst (the S.S. Commander of Lublin camp) and Rachel, one would have to go back into his past. Hans Horst was appointed for his severity and efficiency in clearing ghettos. An Austrian, he had joined the National Socialist party in nineteen thirty two. In nineteen thirty three, he was promoted to the rank of SS Oberschafuhrer (Commissioned Officer) and was put in charge of

Sonder Kommandos, during Special Actions against the Jews. He had earned a reputation of clearing several ghettos, all of which, some seven thousand people, were never seen again. Hans Horst was also the overseer, as well as Commandant for this camp, which was being extended.

Hans Horst had a round chubby figure, wore riding boots, and had a continuous cigar between his lips. Each morning, he would step out of his bungalow, especially built for him by the slave Jewish labourers, and with binoculars, would search out any worker who he considered was malingering, and shoot him or her on sight. The prisoners were hauling big quarry trucks in front of his door. They dare not look his way, or look up at all, in fact, in case they were the subjects of his disfavour. They worked like maniacs for fear of him. Amongst the prisoners was Rachel, who was under the management of the Herr Commandant. There were teams of women, hunched under headscarves, dragging a panel here, a window there; they toiled up and down the slopes under the whips of the Ukrainians, and the instructions of the SS engineers. Barracks were being built, administration huts, the hospital had been completed, for the use of SS and Ukrainian guards. There were forty to fifty women on each team, hauling trolleys of limestones and cement each weighing eight or nine tons. If one of them stumbled or fell, they were kicked and pushed to one side, the momentum must not pause or stop for any individual. Instant execution was the permitted style at this camp. All the women were like living skeletons, and Rachel was no different from the rest.

Her hair had been shaved, but she was allowed to wear a scarf, for the simple reason that the Herr Commandant could not bear to see these ugly women, with sores on their heads, where lice and rats had bitten them. She had been at the camp for about six months, and every day was like a nightmare. She, along with all the other prisoners, was terrified of this man. She had learnt that he had three children, which he adored, two of which were at the front line, fighting for the Fatherland, and that his sexual habits extended from men to women, with frequent beating of the latter.

The prisoners were given a hot substance in the morning, after parole, at noon a cup of barley water, in the evening a piece of bread. She wondered how long she could last, under these circumstances. Her body was frail and thin, but her eyes were like black glowing coals, courage and defiance shone in them; somehow, in some way, she would avenge herself on these murderers. In spite of her gaunt appearance, her beauty could not be stifled or dismissed. It was obvious, that she would not escape from the observation of Hans Horst.

On the tenth day of their arrival, an incident happened, that would mark her for his selections. The camp was overcrowded, with new deportees arriving every day. Hans Horst assembled the prisoners in the women's barracks. 'Jews,' he shouted, 'those of you who have professions, step up.'

There was a pause, they hesitated, having been caught before, they did not know whether they should say yes or no, then one prisoner after another moved forward, stating their professions. Rachel walked forward, and quietly stated, 'I am a nurse.' At the same time, a young beautiful red haired woman advanced and said 'I am a prostitute.'

Rachel admired the disobedience in this girl's stance and quickly, under lowered eyes, looked to see the reaction on the face of the Herr Commandant. There was no reaction, the blue eyes were ice cold in the mild round face.

'Those with professions, form a line to the left,' he said, 'the others to the right.' Rachel joined the queue on the left, and so did the prostitute. 'You,' Hans Horst pointed to the prostitute, 'join the queue to the right.'

The girl bit her lip, and with a slight shrug of her shoulders, obeyed. 'But Herr Commandant,' her voice broke and trembled, 'my profession is as important as the rest.'

'Yes, my beauty, mein liebling,' Hans almost whispered. He sat down, and opening his legs he invited 'Komm, komm to me.'

The girl hesitated, the other prisoners dared not look, they kept their eyes on the floor. The girl looked round contemptuously at the other prisoners, she smiled and swaying her hips, the natural call of her profession, she approached him. Hans took the service revolver from his holster and shot her.

The enormous blast threw the girl against the wall; it was at this moment that Rachel's eyes met the eyes of Hans Holt, a flash of horror and disbelief in hers, and recognition in his; she would be the next to be sorted out, she thought. Under lowered eyes, Rachel watched as the girl's body was carried out of the building.

She did not speak again to the line of prisoners on the right, they just disappeared. She was now no longer under any illusion of what would happen to her. Rachel and her fellow prisoners were there to work until they dropped, or were too ill, or too weak to carry on, then they became no further use to their SS masters.

Rachel could not see a way out. She longed to join the resistance forces, the Jewish organisation ZOB, the activities of which had been whispered from camp to camp, the Jewish partisans who fought within the death camps themselves, but here, there seemed to be no resistance. She saw the look of zombie resemblance on the faces of most of the prisoners, known as Musel Mann. The shoulders sagging, shuffling, with no sense of direction.

It meant that hope had been extinguished, even fight for survival, so important to the Jewish race. Each night, when exhausted from the trials of the day, they were herded into the barracks, and dropped where they stood, too tired to stand, onto bunks, alive with lice and fleas. Rachel remained awake, 'Even with the blade of the sword at your throat, you will not despair of life' she recited the Talmud aloud. The difference was, the Jews who refused to accept the ideas of death, were following this teaching, were submitting, just to stay alive. She would not submit. She tried to rouse the others to fight against the Nazi oppressors, but she received little response, they believed in the lies of their masters. If you worked hard you would be spared, she was told, also with too little food, to sink into a stupor, was all they wanted; to conserve the little strength they had to combat the next day, was all they lived for.

A few days passed, and then, as Rachel knew would happen, she was summoned to present herself before the Commandant. This time, however, the usual suave manner was no longer apparent. Hans Horst was desperately troubled, and his anxiety showed in his face.

'Fraulein,' he rasped, 'I have brought you here for one reason. I have heard it said that you are a nurse, with exceptional skills, particularly your knowledge of skin grafting.' He came straight to the point. 'You are lucky, I have chosen you. Firstly, to nurse my son, who has been shot in our struggle for the Fatherland. His lower jaw has been shot away. You, with your talents, will substitute by plastic surgery, a lower jaw, a further jaw. If you are successful, your abilities will not go unappreciated. If you are not,' the great body shrugged, the sentence remained unfinished.

Rachel saw her chance, 'Mein Commandant,' her eyes met his, 'if I am successful, may I rely on your clemency to release me? I have not committed a crime, I have done no wrong against the state, I just want to return home to my people.'

Hans Horst disliked seeing the hostility in her eyes; his word for it was insubordination, it was as irritating to him as the submissiveness of the rest of them. In fact, this annoyed him even more. He would hit a man to the ground, with the butt of his pistol, just because he was apologetic for not going fast enough in his work, or, for just being apologetic.

Rachel was the type of woman he detested, apart from the fact she was a Jew, she was an educated Jew, a professional Jew, who had the audacity to put herself on his level, not to cower and whimper, as was the expectation, but to stand fearlessly up to him. For the first time, he was not in a position to command. 'Fraulein, my son is awaiting your attention at the hospital. You will be given all that you ask.'

Surviving in these camps for so long, Rachel had not realised that all the men, surgeons, doctors, etc, had been called to the front. She looked at her hands, and wondered if her task was not impossible. Although she had witnessed many a surgical plastic operation whilst she was training, she had never performed such an operation, but, somehow she had to give the impression she knew what she was doing, and then another doubt assailed her, she had not touched nursing implements for nearly three years. Then of course, could she really trust him? Would he keep his word, even if she was successful? He had said she was to be given all that she asked, but that could mean a variety of things, it did not necessarily mean he would give her freedom, and let her go.

Rachel was allowed clean clothes, starched uniform, and a steaming shower. She could not believe her luck, and she luxuriated in the warm water for as long as she dared. She did not think of anything but success.

Hans Horst met her at the hospital doors; 'Follow me,' he ordered, and marched her to the ward where his son was lying. The wards were spotlessly clean, the beds being filled with SS personnel and Ukrainian workers. Rachel turned to the Commandant. 'I need two first class nursing Sisters and an anaesthetist,' she commanded.

The patients were propped up in bed, and they followed her progress in amazement as she pushed a dressing trolley to the bedside of his son Franz. He was also supported by pillows, and she instructed the two nursing Sisters in German, to clean the pulpy mass of his face, where what remained of the structure of his face could be repaired. A sodden dressing covered the lower half of his face, and a piece of gauze fluttered over the trachea, of the lower half of his throat. The anaesthetist arrived, a thoroughly efficient woman, and Rachel ordered the young patient Franz to the operating theatre. She noticed there were no doctors or surgeons to be seen. She did not lose her nerve, however, or her command. She knew her whole life was geared to the success of the operation.

Rachel operated on him for two hours. She removed the dirt and grit of the ditch, and shreds of German uniform from the shapeless mess which was all that remained below his top lip. Her hand did not falter, she dug out the cruel shell splinters and bits of shattered bone, stitching together any skin edges that were left, in order to close the wound. After the operation, she nursed him herself, never leaving his bedside. His eyes alone were enough, for the gratitude he felt for her nursing care. She took down the outer dressings, and with forceps removed the gauze packs from a tongue so swollen and stitched, it was barely recognisable. There was no lower framework to the face, for the jaw had gone. She cleansed the stitch lines and repacked the tongue. His dressings took an hour every day, but she never allowed anyone else to do it, and stayed by his side throughout. Through her steadiness of hand, his jaw could be rebuilt in time.

She was not permitted to talk to her helpers, nor to the patient. It was obvious that they too, were afraid to speak to her, or even look at her. She went on with her work, while SS women patrolled the hospital to see there was no contact. In the hospital, it was warm, civilised; she began to feel like an organised human being again. Every night she was taken back to the camp where there was no warmth. She had looked forward to her daily excursions, and these few days of near freedom. Her task was now completed, and she left the hospital for good, escorted by two Ukrainian guards. When she reached the camp, she was handed sheets of typewritten pink paper. She stared disbelievingly at the paper in her hands. A worker on the food crew smiled encouragingly at her, 'You are free,' he said, 'those pink forms mean release.'

125

Others crowded round shouting congratulations, many of them weeping unashamedly for her. She shook hands with them all, kissing and embracing so many of her comrades. 'The war will soon be over for all of you,' she said. The typewritten form instructed her to be at the main barracks at nine a.m. in the morning.

All night, Rachel lay in a fever of excitement, and was ready and present long before the due time next morning. Her forms were examined and stamped and handed over to a guard. She followed this man into another office. This process lasted all day, as she was shuttled from one room to another, photographed, finger printed. The room began to fill with other prisoners, they lined up, out in the open. She watched happily a bird soar into the air. Soon she would be as free as that bird. The next barracks she entered was a room full of women clerks. Rachel was handed a paper bag, full of her personal items. Her nurse's brooch, watch, her cap and apron, neatly starched and ironed, her wedding ring that she loved so much, she put it lovingly on her hand. She was marched to a further barracks marked 'A'. Before a bored clerk, she was told to pass her personal effects at the window on the opposite side.

'But I have just been handed them,' she said, 'my papers say I am to be released.'

The bored clerk chose to ignore her remarks, and repeated his sentence, 'Jewellery, watches, rings.'

Rachel moved to the opposite window, numb with shock. She took off her brooch and her wedding ring, and handed them in.

'Next,' said a uniformed figure. Sick with disappointment, the fortitude she had shown for so long began to crack; she was convulsed with sobs that shook her thin frame.

'Form lines, schnell,' the usual technique for maintaining discipline. The guards shrieked obscenities, and screamed at their prisoners. So, they had deceived her, after all, and their gratitude could be the end for her, because now she had become an embarrassment to them.

'Prisoners halt, form lines,' a florid official formed them into a double column and marched all the prisoners, including Rachel, back to the main barracks. The whole episode was a farce, and she recognised the fact. She was determined, however, not to concede without a fight; she must somehow rouse the others from their lethargy.

That night, back amongst the sighs and stirrings of hundreds of women, she began to fight, with all the energy she could muster. She was fitter now, she had been given good food when conducting the operation on the son of Hans Horst, and with her energy came an inner force and strength.

'Friends,' she cried, 'you know that all Jews driven away are led to their death.'

There was silence, she repeated her sentence louder. The older women shouted, 'That is not true, don't listen to her, she is a trouble maker, go back to sleep,' they had decided to play the comedy of hope. They were too old to accept the truth; the younger women collected around

Rachel, their eyes never leaving her face. Rachel was unnerved by the reaction of the elders.

'Each of us is under the sentence of death; we have nothing to lose,' she stated, 'Fight them, even with your bare hands, grab their guns, their pistols, their machine-guns, don't be led away like sheep going to slaughter. Even if we are too weak to defend our lives, we are strong enough to defend our Jewish honour, and human dignity, even if it means suicide. Prove to the world we did not go freely to our death. Fight for your life, with tooth and nail, axe and knife. Make them pay for our blood, death with death.'

She paused, even this speech had taken a lot of her energy. Her cry for salvation though, had not gone unheard. A young blonde woman, standing beside Rachel, took up her appeal, shouting above the uproar, 'How can we fight against machine guns?'

Rachel quietly resumed her speech, like an actress overcoming an audience, who rose as one to an ovation, she knew they would follow her command, there was no other option. 'The war cannot continue forever, somewhere there is another life from this; where the world can become a clean and happy place and we can live normal lives, without continuous fear. Many of us will die in our fight for freedom, but, with our overwhelming numbers, they will not be expecting our onslaught, so when I call out NOW, fall on them, grab their guns and shoot. Do not hesitate, then run like mad to the forests that surround the camp, with the arms of the murderers you have just killed.' There was now uproar in the barracks. 'Time for me is running out,' Rachel continued, 'Our masters will be told by some of you, the weak among you, of what I have said, but when I call NOW,' she repeated, 'follow me and do as I do.' This was followed by a roar of assertion.

It was a long time before the women finally settled down to sleep, they talked for hours in whispers, plan after plan was discussed, but for them, Rachel was their leader and their hope. She knew, within a few hours, that one or the other had betrayed her to the Nazis. At six the next morning, they heard the camp was to be razed to the ground. The Germans took great pains to see that nothing leaked to the outside world.

The exodus began, they stumbled through a maze of barbed wire, onto the rough road, which ended in front of a single rail track, where a train was awaiting them. Machine-guns were mounted, at intervals, beside the road. Soldiers were approaching along the track, to haul open the heavy sliding doors. They were prodded into the train by the soldiers. The small car was becoming crowded, enough room for thirty or forty people, and still the soldiers crowded them in, with shrieks arising from inside the car. The women were packed in so tightly, they could hardly breathe, they heard the iron bolts driven into place. Then they were sobbing and fainting. The air became foul. Rachel started to tug at a nail, in the ancient wood of the wall of the train. Others helped her and soon there were blessed whiffs of air, circulating round the whole compartment. The train gave a sudden lurch and began to move.

The day came and went, as she looked through the hole she had made, Rachel saw they were passing through the town of Plaszow, Auschwitz was to be their destination, then. The word went round the train, passing from mouth to mouth, a word of doom.

Eventually, the train stopped, and the door slid open; they crawled out, like infants, on hands and knees. They could scarcely walk, but they were ready for the word 'NOW'. They were not allowed to talk, but their eyes expressed a world of meaning. Rachel shook her head, not yet she mouthed silently. They formed into straggly columns, by the shore of a blue glistening lake, and were marched away. They struggled past the lake and up a hill. At the top of the hill, looking down, they saw low grey barracks, with concrete walls and barbed wire. So this was Auschwitz. As they approached this evil place, they saw the skull and crossbones posted, on barbed wire, to enable the prisoners to know that the fence was electrified.

The massive gates opened to this bedraggled group. Through a loud speaker, with a swinging military band in the background, disorganised and off key, the Jews were assured their belongings could be reclaimed, as soon as they had been through the decontamination process; Rachel knew what a selection meant, fortunately for most of them they were blindly ignorant. There were about a dozen SS doctors.

One of them stared at her, with red fugitive eyes, as if sleep had forever left him, he muttered, 'It is sad, you are so beautiful.' He was like a medieval archangel, and in his hands was a whip with many strands, which he indolently and indifferently flicked from left to right. His power was absolute, and he administered death in the same way as a waitress would serve vegetables on a plate, and just as indifferently.

Rachel was very afraid, she had heard so often in the past, these stories of terror, almost unbelievable, but here she was in front of this doctor, awaiting his signal, for life or death; she hoped the women behind her would support her when she cried out. Her moment had come, with thudding heart she swayed, as hunger and nausea overcame her, and this it seemed was her undoing. He had made a decision on her fitness. Those he considered fit for work, he waved to the left. The unfit, elderly people and children were all waved to the right, bolstered up with plausible promises, that no harm would befall them, the older would look after the younger, as it were. The whip hovered in the air for one agonising second, all eyes followed it, and it fell to the right. So they were going to kill her, after all, but not without a fight she determined.

Fate again took a hand, the doctor's aide, a waxy skinned Rotten Fuhrer, stepped up to her, relaxing his guard for one moment. He was so attracted to her beauty, he wanted a better look. As he did so, at that precise moment, she grabbed his hip revolver, shouting at the same time 'NOW' she shot him dead. Instantaneously, the women, mustering whatever strength they had left, fell on their Nazi monsters, with sheer weight of numbers killing the doctors and several of their henchmen, by grabbing their guns and running as fast as they could for the safety of the woods, or for anything that gave them shelter. It was a fight to the finish, they knew that from the beginning, but they did not die in vain.

Chapter Nine

Stacey's Story

Stacey ran and ran, her face and hands were cut and bleeding, sustained in throwing herself out through the hospital window. The tommy gun she had grabbed in the struggle was heavy enough, but she did not notice either the heaviness of the gun, nor the cut over her eye, which was bleeding profusely and covering her face with blood. Every now and then, when blinded by the blood, she dashed her hand over her face, to clear her sight, hardly pausing in the procedure.

She must have covered six or seven kilometres before she stopped suddenly, to take stock of her surroundings and her situation. The visual carnage she had left behind, the look of surprise on the German soldier's face, would stay with her for ever. The killing of Joseph and Sergeant Thompson, she could hardly believe she had been party to this horror. It had to be eliminated or she would go mad. Stacey paused, her breath coming in gasps, she took great gulps of air, the calming procedure for panic; these instructions she had so often given patients, now she needed this advice for herself. She sank to her knees, trying to control the hysteria that overcame her. Her reasoning had not left her, though; she had carefully avoided all roads, keeping to fields and woods. If she directed herself north, she thought, she must eventually come to the sea with the possibility of escaping to England, as long as she was not caught.

Her mind now became very active. She went over her assets. Taking out all the belongings in the pockets of her uniform, a few francs, matches, thermometer, and a watch clipped onto her breast pocket, useful walking shoes, and the nurse's cap, which could be turned into a scarf. Stacey threw away her starched collar and cuffs, and in her light grey dress, could look like any French girl, going about her business.

But the problem was the gun, it was her only protection. She undid her cape, wrapping the gun around it. She had to face the unpleasant facts, of no money, no food, no protective clothing, and more than important, no credentials, only a smattering of French, likely to be informed on, and turned over to the Police at any time. In fact, she was at the mercy of one and all. On top of this negative thinking, it started to rain. She must keep running however by night, sleeping by day, as long as there was an ever widening gap between the hospital and herself. This was the only thought, to get away, to escape.

Stacey stopped again, exhausted, she had no idea where she was. It stopped raining, in the broken moonlight she perceived a shack in a clearing of a glade; she was wet and shivering. At least, it could shelter her for the night, she could not advance any further anyway, she was collapsing with fatigue. The death of her friends seemed meaningless now, remote and far-away, nothing had any sense. Stacey cautiously circled the shack, leaning against the wooden structure, she peered through the broken glass of the window, then coming to the door, she kicked it open. The door gave way easily to her weight. The barn was empty, except for a mound of wood and twigs, piled high in the corner. Her matches in her pocket were comparatively dry, and with no further ado, she dragged some twigs in the middle of the floor and attempted to light them. Her hands were trembling with the exertion, as one match after another lit, and fizzled out, but, luck was with her, she managed to coax the twigs into a reasonable fire.

Stacey took off her dress, pants and bra, and started to dry her clothes, turning this way and that way, at the same time trying to warm herself, she came as close to the flames as she could. Eventually, her dress and underclothes started to produce dry patches, as she fed the fire with further twigs, and as soon as they were dry, she dressed. Making an uncomfortable pillow with the gun and cape under her head, she curled into a ball and fell asleep.

Stacey could not have been asleep for any length of time, when she was instantly awakened and aware of danger, by whisperings and movement at the other end of the barn. Stacey grabbed the gun, underneath her head, but at the same time, her face was caught in the bright dazzling light of a large torch. It was impossible to see who was shining the torch. Assuming sleep, through half closed eyes, she could make out two or three filthy dark bundled figures, smelling of booze.

They encircled her, muttering together in French. 'C'est lui, je vous diz. Celui une ils cherchent, la nourrice. ('It's her, I tell you. The one they are looking for, the nurse they are searching for.')

The other figure, answered, going over her body with the torch, meticulously, 'Je pense, vous avez raison, et il sera bon pour 'two francs' biensior.' ('I think you are right. We can make a couple of bob over this.')

'Comment?' enquired the third figure, at the same time taking a swig from his bottle; 'N'importe. Laisse celui a Georges.' ('Never mind. Leave it to George.')

The first scallywag answered secretly, touching his nose. They withdrew, putting out the torch, going into a huddle, with further murmurings in French. Stacey jumped to her feet, pointing the gun at them, they turned to her, momentarily amazed and confused, they were not expecting her to be armed. She could just make out their forms in the glowing embers of the dying fire.

'Beat it,' said Stacey, making a determined movement with the gun, should they try to get nearer. She reddened, correcting herself, 'I mean Allez.' Her finger, menacingly on the trigger of the gun. The leader of the clan, known it seemed by the others, by name of George, advanced like an evil crow.

'Mais, Madame,' he said gently, then in English 'you have the catch on.' He repeated this in French to the other two, which was hailed in merriment, they fell about, roaring uproariously with laughter. Stacey looked quickly down at the gun, colouring with annoyance. In this slight hesitation, Georges made a dart for the gun, but, just as quickly she shot a volley of bullets into the roof of the barn.

Georges jumped back in fear, 'Merd alors' he swore, and they stared at her, in alarm and a new respect. They again went into a huddle, looking back over their shoulders at her, whispering together. Georges, who was obviously their leader, indicated to the others in French, 'A se rompre. Celui d'aller a gauche, et l'autre en droite.' ('Split up, one to go to her left, and the other to her right.') Still keeping his distance, seeing how excited she had become, he decided to use diplomacy. 'Inglishe,' he said, using gentle persuasion, 'Where you get the gun? You are prisoner, yes, running away from the Germans?'

'Yes, you are right,' she replied, gruffly, 'I stole it from the Germans, I shot as many as I could and ran for it.' Strangely enough, this statement was almost true. Stacey ranged the gun from right to left, and back again. She looked at them, to see if they believed her. The three scarecrows were definitely impressed, they sat on their haunches, never taking their eyes away from her, still keeping a respectful distance. Georges, lightening the situation, but not giving up his hold on her, said, 'We make friends, yes. This is Jean,' introducing the most alcoholic of the lot, 'Shake the lady by the hand,' he added, kicking him at the same time. Jean staggered drunkenly over to Stacey, wiping his grimy hand on his over large overcoat grinning sheepishly, 'Bonjour Madame!'

Stacey backed, as far as possible, 'Keep your distance,' she shouted, 'we can be friends, but keep away from me.'

Jean looked at George, disconcerted. 'We can also turn you over to the Police,' Georges insinuated, softly.

'No, that would be stupid,' she guessed correctly, 'they want you, as much as they want me.'

That did it, they turned away from her, Georges shouted at the third desperado, whose name turned out to be Luc, aiming a kick at him, 'Luc, make a fire.'

Luc and Jean scurried away obeying his slightest wish. Stacey could see he was the boss. As the fire burned brighter, they could see each other better. They sat in front of her, on their haunches, gazing at her, speculatively, leering with toothless grins.

Georges turned to Stacey, 'Inglishe, we know who you are. You are the missing nurse. No good. We find other clothes for you, we let you stay with us, yes, but you must work, you must work for us.'

Stacey again tightened her grip on the gun; she must not sleep, whatever happened, she must keep awake, otherwise they would seize the gun and maybe herself, as well. 'I work for no-one,' she spoke arrogantly. 'I am going home.'

This caused further guffaws, 'Home, what's that?' they cried, falling about drunkenly. Luc brought out his mouth organ, playing a rendering of 'Home, sweet home on the range' which they joined in, singing enthusiastically.

'You're mad,' said Georges, 'how can you get home?'

'I don't know,' said Stacey, 'somehow.'

'Inglishe, you have no home, you will never get back. If you are caught, you know what happens'…Georges made an impromptu gesture, of slitting his throat. 'But,' he continued, 'you can cook for us, and nurse us.'

Fooling about, they worked out a quick pantomime, one holding the wrist of the other, as a nurse with a patient, dancing closer all the time. They then changed tactics, bringing out a rucksack, they passed food to each other, bread and a bottle of wine. Stacey watched them hungrily, she was famished. Georges could see her hunger. 'Give us the gun, then you can eat.'

'No,' shouted Stacey.

Georges shrugged, 'Inglishe, it is up to you. We now sleep, you sleep, too. In the morning we work,' with that, the three settled down in their tattered clothes to sleep, and in time, they were all snoring in unison. Try as she could to keep awake, the warmth of the fire, and the terror she had left behind, was too much for Stacey, her lids became heavy, her head drooped. Every now and then, she would half wake, re-seize the gun, but, within seconds, her head drooped again, she was fast asleep.

Stacey was jerked awake by a bundle of greasy clothes being thrown at her, accompanied by a battered straw hat, and basket. Georges was standing watching her, and now she could see them for what they were, and a more dangerous set of ruffians she was yet to find. They did not avert their eyes as she dressed, and they appraised her in French, slyly looking at her, and each other, as she slipped the skirt over her nurse's dress, and the blouse which usefully buttoned up to her neck.

'Pas mal, dans une nuit tenebreuse,' said Jean. (Not bad on a dark night.) They laughed.

Georges did not turn away his gaze. 'Hier soir, nous avons manque chance, helas! Quelle volupte nous pourons avoir lui donne! Elle nous remercerait.' (We had a chance last night, we should have taken it. We could have given her a good time, she would have thanked us) he said boastfully.

'Trop enivres' (Too drunk) said Luc.

Stacey was mercifully glad the gun was still wrapped round the cape. She wriggled out of her uniform, pulled on the boots that were given to her, and with a flourish banged on the battered hat. She hated the gun, it was heavy, cumbersome and a nuisance to carry, she would have liked to have thrown it away, but she did not dare. She kept the basket over her left arm, and laid the gun at the bottom, covering it with her uniform. In training, she was skilled in unarmed silent combat, taught by the erstwhile Sergeant Thompson, but she could not take chances. By supporting the basket in her right hand, she was able to keep her left hand on the trigger, if necessary.

Georges brought her hot coffee, with chunks of bread for all of them. 'Inglishe,' he called, 'my friends, my familee say 'ello.'

Through the cracked pane of the window, she saw hordes of French peasants and children surrounding the shack, all pushing each other in their efforts to catch a glimpse of this English nurse.

'Gawd!' said Stacey, 'the whole world is here.'

They all came to gaze on her, as if she was a monkey in a zoo. It must have gone round the village like wild fire, she thought, that George had found an English nurse. In no time, the Police would know, then the Gestapo would pick her up, and the game would be up. But there was nothing she could do, but to go along with it.

'Now, we work,' said Georges, and en mass they all trooped out of the barn, to the maize fields, potato furrows, and vineyards. As soon as she emerged, she was surrounded by the curious onlookers, gabbling questions in French to her and at her. Stacey realised how clever George had been, and how cleverly he had hidden her. The children danced round her, touching the basket whenever they dared, asking endless questions of what was in the basket, and could they carry the basket for her.

'Non, allez. Piss off,' said the irritated Stacey. Stacey often swore, her explanation being, that she had worked with the Army all her life, so it was second nature to her, and not her fault. The peasants surrounded Stacey hiding her amongst them, they all started to sing, as they marched down to the vineyards. When they arrived Georges turned to her, in his insolent way, 'Mind you keep your mouth shut. If anyone questions you, Inglishe, demanding papers, then you are deaf and dumb, yes? and we tell them, you deaf and dumb. They give up quickly, they non comprez your signs.' He showed her a few complicated signs, the children screamed with laughter.

'I no comprez them either,' said Stacey.

Georges laughed and turned away from her. 'Start work,' he ordered the crowd. Stacey looked intently at the orderly groves of sweet oranges, the vineyards, smelling the sweet air of luscious fruit, and moved towards the potato patch still clutching her basket. She watched Georges as he directed the procedure, admiring his organisation. Everyone had a specific job to do, and within minutes the whole vineyard was buzzing with activity. Georges came over to her, 'Inglishe, you dig here, fill your basket, and pour the potatoes into that bin,' he indicated a large bin, then whispering 'Give me your gun, if they catch you with it,' he again draws his finger across his neck.

'No,' said Stacey stubbornly.

Georges shrugged, 'Don't say I did not warn you.' Turning on the others 'What are you standing about for? Dig for victory.'

Stacy dropped onto her knees, thrusting her hands deep into the earth feeling about, she found several potatoes, stuffing them into her basket, covering the gun with them. She decided to work on a stretch of twenty feet or so. She noticed the three ruffians kept close surveillance on her, surrounding her, never leaving her out of their sight, they grin, cheering her on to better efforts. She could not understand why Georges had said 'Dig for victory'. Victory for whom, the Germans? There was something funny going on, she could not put her finger on it.

The sun rose in the sky, she became hotter and hotter, wiping the sweat off her face. Her clothes were heavy, smelling horribly. Stacey finished two rows of potatoes and was turning to her third, when she looked up again to find there was no one to be seen; the children had gone, the ruffians had disappeared. From afar, at the edge of the field, she perceived the reason for their disappearance.

She saw two German soldiers, together with a Policeman, staring suspiciously at her. Why hadn't the others warned her? Her heart began beating with terror. How could I have been so stupid, so engrossed in what I was thinking? she thought to herself. There was no other way, but to bluff it out, and resort to the sign language suggested by Georges or to blast her way out with the gun. Still keeping her fingers on the trigger, she strolled as casually as she could, taking out the potatoes throwing them one by one into the bin. She saw the Police pointing to her, visibly arguing with each other, then having made up their minds, they firmly approached her. They were coming towards her, there was no doubt about that.

Panic seized her, she turned in the opposite direction, as if a thought had just occurred to her. A worker who had been studiously collecting oranges in the orange grove, had been watching the tense situation between Stacey and the Police. He calmly descended from the tree, throwing his oranges into a basket, at the bottom of the tree. As she passed under the tree, without hesitating, he put his arm round her shoulders, swinging her towards him, and nibbling her ear.

He whispered menacingly 'Pass your basket to me.'

She started to protest, only to feel the cold steel of a knife in her ribs. There was nothing to do but to obey.

'Start laughing,' he hissed, 'put your arm through mine, look as if you love me. When I run, you chase me, follow me.' They played an intriguing game in front of the Police and the Germans. The peasant ran round the trees and she followed laughing. He never allowed her to catch him however but all the time he headed for the woods. In the end, he put his arm round her waist leading her away, as if for lunch. She slipped her arm round his waist. He gave a backward glance, the Police were no longer interested, they were talking amongst themselves.

When they arrived under the shelter of the trees, they ran like startled deer. He never relaxed his pressure, as he pushed her forward, the world was spinning, she was gasping for breath, on and on, never stopping for one moment. Sometimes they wallowed in mud, well over their ankles, scrambling up hills, clinging on to roots, anything that would hold the weight of their bodies, deep into woods that thickened and turned into forests. They kept well away from roads that had been hewed through the trees. At times they spotted the flash of headlights, as lorries and German tanks rumbled through the woods.

There were times when the peasant halted their fleeing progress; in so doing, he would take a bottle of wine from a shoulder bag, take a swig from the bottle, then wiping the mouth of the bottle, he would pass it to Stacey, she would do likewise passing it back to him. They moved at night, and hid by day, snatching sleep whenever they could, resting their exhausted bodies.

Time stood still. Once she was awakened sharply by a group of German soldiers marching through the woods; they were so close, she could have put out her hand and touched them. She grabbed the machine gun which lay by the side of her companion, but the incident passed, they had been well hidden by foliage.

On about the third day, the man halted, and taking a scarf from his pocket, he commanded her to turn round. 'Come here,' he said.

'Why?' said the suspicious Stacey.

'I am going to blindfold you, then, I will turn you round three times.' He proceeded to blindfold Stacey, turning her round three times. He guided her for several minutes, then he let her go.

'Hey, where are you?' Stacey stumbled nearly falling. She snatches off the blindfold, the man was nowhere to be seen.

Chapter Ten

Stacey found herself standing at an entrance of a cave. An opening of large dimension, or an uprooting of a tree, blown down, maybe, well hidden from road or air, and there to greet her were the three rascally tramps she had met in the shack previously.

Georges grinned in his usual insolent way, 'Bonjour, Inglishe,' accompanied with a leer, 'Meet your comrades in arms in resistance.' They seemed to be guarding the way to the entrance. As he spoke he was joined by two or three, mainly unkempt individuals, a thoroughly unruly lot. They look at her curiously, but there was no welcome in their greeting. A man stepped forward and whispered hurriedly to Georges, who nodded his head in assent, and turning to Stacey, 'Inglishe, we take you to meet our leader and commander.'

Taking her hand, he pulled her into the hole. A narrow passage led the way to a larger cave. Georges pushed her through this passage, well lit with oil lamps.

Stacey realised immediately who they were. They were the famous Resistance fighters founded in 1940. This little group joined with other small resistance groups all over France, forming the well known network named 'Combat' and 'Le Maquis'. She had heard about them many times before. In the hospital, cafes, shops, the name had been whispered about everywhere.

Stacey was amazed by the hum of activity that greeted her, as she entered the larger cave. On all sides, the Resistance were effectively forging identity papers, essential for the freedom of resistance workers, ration cards, Molotov cocktails, made by saboteurs from every day material such as bottles and tins. As she passed another section, she saw a radio operator tapping out Morse code messages. His section had been sunk into the ground in the form of a square, which enabled only one person to operate the proceedings, also presumably to cut noise and the brisk energies around him.

Georges waved cheerily to the Resistance fighters as he passed them with Stacey. He was obviously liked and trusted by them. They acknowledged him, but briefly, they were solely concerned with their work. They came eventually to a rough wooden door. Georges respectfully knocked discreetly.

A slit in the door opened briefly. Georges whispered 'Combat,' whereby the door opened revealing a hooded masked figure. Georges thrust her forward, and with a click of heels he said 'Your prisoner, sir' then saluting smartly, he withdrew, closing the door behind him.

The room was bare of essentials, except for a table, three chairs, behind which lay a detailed staff map of France, sectioned into exact positions of Wehrmacht units. This map took the space of a whole wall, marked with the proficiency of a military mind. The owner of which confronted her with strict demeanour. The room was full of smoke, both by cigarettes, and oil lamps producing and emitting smoke.

Stacey could just ascertain three figures, all sitting behind the desk. In the middle, between two hooded men, sat an English Officer, wearing Infantry Combat uniform. He introduced himself as Captain Anderson. On the bridge of his nose sat a pair of rimless spectacles, giving the cold eyes a glittering appearance. He proffered her a chair, there was a momentary silence, as he subjected her to close scrutiny.

Then with quick icy precision, he embarked on a tirade of controlled fury. He made it quite plain, the reason why she had been brought in front of him. It must be clearly understood by her, that she had been saved from the Gestapo, or worse, not because she was a stranded English woman in France, they were not interested in that, but, because she was a nurse, or so he had been led to believe. 'Where is your identity, and why you are wandering about in the middle of enemy occupied territory with no papers?'

Stacey answered as well as she could, but even to her, her excuses seemed pretty lame and feeble. She faltered defensively, 'I am a Sister attached to the Queen Alexandra Military Unit. We should have caught the hospital train to Boulogne sur Mer, but we were bombed at Abbeville station and in the confusion we were left behind.'

'Left behind,' Captain Anderson spluttered, 'how could you be left behind? Were you the only one?'

'No, there were three of us.'

Intercepting this harsh exchange of words were moans of someone or something in a room nearby, someone in a great deal of pain. Captain Anderson remained oblivious of this, continuing questioning, cross examining, interrogating, his eyes never leaving her face. He enjoyed making people afraid of him. 'Where are these three now?'

' I don't know,' she retorted.

'You are a fool, if you think I believe your story, left behind, indeed. Up to something you shouldn't have been, no doubt.'

Stacey replied hotly 'We were finding food for refugee children.'

He made her feel very small, stupid and humiliated. Captain Anderson continued doggedly 'It is not your place to find food. It was your duty to look after your patients. You have betrayed your trust and disobeyed your commanding officer, your Matron. I take this breach of duty very seriously. At your age, you should have known better. You will be reported.'

Stacey coloured, she was not a person to be browbeaten, she replied testily, 'What point is there in reporting me? Who will you report me to?'

'Don't be clever with me,' he replied sharply, he could hardly contain his irritation, 'Now, you will listen to me, and listen good. This war will not last for ever, we are all fighting to rid the enemy from this shore,' then ponderously, 'You have the choice. Join our group, or be turned out of here, unceremoniously. There will be no return, you will have to find your own way back to England, I doubt if you will ever get there. If you want to stay alive,' he warned, 'you must obey precisely everything I command you to do. I do not tolerate disobedience, and that means everything, without the slightest hesitation or even thought. Personally I don't like women mixed in the fighting force, it is not their place. The home, looking after children, is their rightful position in life, but under these circumstances we have no choice. From now on, you will become a member of our fighting force, but, remember, if you get caught, you are on your own, the reprisals are savage. My men have risked their lives trying to save you from the Germans, I would have let you go to the devil myself, but I was outvoted.'

Throughout this exchange of words, the groans in the adjoining room were getting louder.

'Take note,' he went on, 'this conversation has never taken place, we do not exist, you understand.'

'I am not a traitor,' said Stacey stoutly.

'That is easy to say now, but under torture, it is a different proposition.' Captain Anderson suddenly burst out laughing.

He enjoys making me afraid of him, thought Stacey and then laughs at my fears. The interview was over. Captain Anderson stood up, rounded the table and putting an arm on her shoulder, said calmly, 'The reason I need you, I must be honest, is because one of my men, Hans, has appendicitis. If you can not help him, he will die, as surely as that.'

'But,' faltered Stacey, '…I have never performed an operation in my life.' Alarm spread all over her face.

'Well, now's your chance. What are you waiting for?' said Captain Anderson casually. With that, he strode into a sparsely furnished ante room. The two masked men followed, with Stacey trailing in their wake.

The anteroom was full of smoke, not only from paraffin lamps, but also from cigarettes, being smoked by the Resistance. Lying on a rough table is a man of Swedish/Danish appearance. He is surrounded by Resistance fighters of all descriptions. Poles, French, Dutch, Belgians all jabbering in their own language. The man is very drunk, and is liberally supplied with whisky, whenever he demands it. The man is moaning, and is in great pain. The Resistance were not particularly sympathetic to his moans. Between his legs, that are sprawled out on the table, they were playing cards, betting and quarrelling, amongst themselves.

Stacey bent over the man, known as Hans, and turning to Captain Anderson, she said, 'I cannot help this man, he needs to be in hospital.'

'Use your sense, woman,' was the rude reply, 'if he goes to hospital, he will never survive, he will be cornered by the Germans, tortured and killed. You're a nurse aren't you?'

'Yes,' stuttered Stacey.

'Well, get on with it then. Get cracking.'

Stacey glared at him, if they were in different circumstances, she would have slapped his face, as it was she had to tolerate his insults. It was at this point Stacey noticed a young woman, sobbing quietly in the corner. She must have been twenty or thereabouts. She was in a state of great anxiety, twisting her handkerchief into knots. No one took a blind bit of notice of her, however.

Captain Anderson took control. 'Men,' he said, 'this woman is Sister Scott, she will be joining our group. I shall expect you to find exactly what she requires, for an operation on our friend, here.'

Stacey looked down at the man, then hesitatingly, she said, 'This man is to be shaved.'

The Resistance looked dubiously at Stacey, then at Captain Anderson for instruction. 'Well, you heard her,' he said.

Stacey took command. 'I need a scalpel, thin knife, sponge holders, artery forceps, retractors, swabs, drapes, gloves, antiseptic lotion, boiling water, a gown for myself; I will need an assistant who will also need gloves and gown.'

One of the men had written down her instructions on his hand. Georges came up to her, 'I will be your assistant,' he said quietly. 'Give me one hour, and I will bring you everything you need.' He handed her a hot tin mug of sweet tea. Stacey looked at him, sceptically, 'You, Georges?'

'Yes, Inglishe.'

She noticed his dirty finger nails, his unkempt appearance, but she said nothing. 'Hurry please and thanks.' She turned to the others, 'Scrub down this table with carbolic soap, or any soap.' She helped them to lie the patient on the floor, and grabbing a bucket she started scrubbing down the table, drinking tea, intermittently. There was another lull in the proceedings. The Resistance were not used to taking orders from a woman, they again looked to Captain Anderson for their orders.

'Please,' said Stacey, 'I want you to think of me as one of yourselves. Treat me as a man.'

Captain Anderson began to like this woman, the way she handled the men, her authority. 'Get on with it,' he barked.

There was a general whirl about, with her orders being obeyed explicitly. Somewhere they found a knife, and antiseptic lotion. 'Shave him, please' she reiterated as soon as the table had been scrubbed, and Hans had been returned onto it again. Georges returned with all the necessary equipment. How he obtained it, she did not know, it occurred to her that he probably robbed a nearby hospital. 'Sterilise all instruments' she commanded.

Georges was dressed and gowned with clean hands and nails, combed hair, beard straightened. Stacey could hardly believe it was the same man, she could even see what he looked like, now. In an undertone to Georges, Stacey expressed her fear of the operation but Georges refused to listen.

'Inglishe, You'll win. I know you will. How can you not succeed with Georges beside you,' he said, encouragingly.

Stacey bent over Hans, cleaning his skin with antiseptic lotion. The Resistance fighters crowded round the table, watching her every movement. The man was very drunk, she would have to perform the operation without anaesthetic. 'I need boiling water, and as much light as possible.' The men brought in further paraffin lamps, which smoked profusely. 'We have no time to lose,' she said, 'but if you want to help, I want very clean hands, now.'

They again rushed in all directions, spotless hands were shown to her. 'Now, cover him with drapes, but leave the lower part of the abdomen exposed. Secure the drapes with towel clips.' She took a deep breath, the Resistance gathered round, 'Give me some room, dammit.' They stepped back temporarily, but surged forward almost immediately. 'Give him another swig of whisky,' said Stacey, anxiously.

Captain Anderson came round to the opposite side of the table. 'Now, my friend,' he said to Hans, 'We are all doing what we can for you. There is no pain to it, just a slight prick and it will all be over. It is your duty to pull yourself together, as quickly as possible, so you can join us again, as a fighting force, anything else is sabotage.'

The man opened drunken eyes and moaned.

'Well, here goes,' said Stacey, trying to conceal the tremble in her voice and hands. Stacey made an incision with the knife. Hans made an almighty yell, 'Hold him down,' she was losing her nerve, 'keep him still.' But the man was thrashing about, and screaming, blood was spurting everywhere. 'Knock him out,' she commanded. A tall bearded fighter came over swiftly and hit the jaw of Hans. The man collapsed like a pricked balloon.

Stacey was shaking, she had not expected this turn of events, somehow, she had to keep her hand from shaking. 'Ligatures.' Georges handed them to her. She took another deep breath; she cut through the fat, and tied off the bleeding vessels with catgut ligatures. 'Knife.'

She worked quickly and simply. It was not easy with the men bending over, watching the scene. Every now and then, she pushed them away with her elbow. In an English hospital, they would have a fit if they saw her now. She would not be allowed or even thought of, for such an arduous task. She cut through the muscle, and extended her incision. 'Scissors' she called.

She found the appendix, and isolated it. Once isolated, she asked Georges to hold the tissue forceps, on the tip of the appendix; Stacey was now in charge of the situation. She divided the blood vessels, tied them off with catgut. There was a deep silence, one could hear a pin drop. She then counted carefully all her swabs, so that none were left inside the patient. 'I am closing the muscle, threading the needle, and stitching the incision.' With a satisfied sigh, 'It is finished.' Stacey looked up, they were all grinning at her. She smiled, thanking them for their help. 'With careful nursing, I think he will pull through.'

Captain Anderson was the first to congratulate her. 'Well done, congratulations.' With those words all pandemonium broke out. The men laughed, slapping Stacey, and each other on the back. You would think they had performed the operation.

'I could not have succeeded without your help,' said Stacey, modestly. This brought forth further cheers and admiration.

'Now, we must leave our heroine to get some sleep.' Captain Anderson was very pleased with her efforts. 'Miss Scott,' he said, 'I presume you have made your decision to stay with us, we could do with a person of your qualities in our team.'

Stacey said stoutly 'Sir, I am very proud to be with you all, and I will do my very best.'

'You will do better than that, my dear.'

No one could get big headed with Captain Anderson, he always had the last word, that was his style. Georges took her hand, 'Cheers, Inglishe, now we go to bed, but not with me tonight, Josephine,' he said, with his usual insolent grin.

Stacey was incredibly happy, she had been accepted, and earned the respect of the whole group of Resistance including Captain Anderson.

On the whole, his view of women was chauvinistic. He had the old fashioned idea, that their place was in the home, providing for men, but he made an exception in Stacey. Being female, though, was no excuse; she would not be treated any differently than the men. If she cracked under their vigorous training, he would have had no hesitation in turning her out, to fend for herself in this hostile country. She had, after all, fulfilled her requirements, and it meant another mouth to feed. He decided to bide his time, in assessing her value, and to give her work of a dangerous nature, to test whether she could stand up to the experiment.

Stacey was now a volunteer of the Resistance. She had absolutely no preparation for what she did. She was not a soldier like the other Resistance fighters; she was thrown into the Resistance without any weapons, as security of weapons was one thing, but Combat units often trained with broom handles, whilst waiting to acquire weapons. All she had, was complete faith in Captain Anderson. Training was intensive and vigorous. First she was entered into the school of sabotage. She learned how to fire guns, how to become an accomplished thief, how to conduct sabotage, including 'silent killing'. They set to work to teach her the deaf and dumb language. She was given strict instructions never to speak, and never to talk in English. She had to learn her cover story in deaf and dumb language. They forged a medical card stating this information, and supplied identity papers, so she could move around easily.

The Resistance were in constant need for food, plus food coupons. Many of the Resistance group were sons of the local shopkeepers, who were well aware of the mission of their sons, therefore, they turned a blind eye in supplying them with goods, without books or coupons. The owners of the local shops never felt it necessary to discuss the risk of supplying food to those pursued by the enemy. But, on the other hand, the shopkeepers were quite often less than pleased to contribute to the Resistance, when it intervened with their black market dealings.

The Resistance fighters were up every morning at 6 a.m. Captain Anderson commanded them, as if in the Army. Once out of the school, Stacey had further advanced teachings, with the others, in the use of codes, shooting, sabotage etc. She liked this life, the camaraderie, the roughness, the excitement, dicing with death. She now moved in the shifting, dangerous world of the Resistance.

Make no mistake about it, the Gestapo with cancerous method, fastened on small groups, then destroyed them, and in eliminating them, shot anyone who was in any way suspect. Many innocent people lost their lives in this way, caught up in Gestapo nets. The Germans had the largest Intelligence Service and Counter Intelligence in the world.

Captain Anderson continued to be an enigma to Stacey. Easy going as he was to his men, he was quite the opposite to Stacey, and one or two of the other women agents. Cold and icy, he treated them as if they were unintelligent, slow witted, and shouldn't be there. He, and other heads of the Resistance, would take on the roles of Gestapo men, which gave them all an idea of the rigorous interrogation they could expect if caught. Behind it, was to break them and their cover stories. These rehearsals were grim affairs. They would round up the recruits in the same way as the Gestapo, and order them to strip naked under blazing spotlights, women as well as men.

Stacey would stand for hours, whilst they questioned her in deaf and dumb language.

'Name' barked an authorised Resistant. Stacey replied very slowly in deaf and dumb fashion.

'Where are you residing?'

Stacey replied correctly in the answers that she had learnt, but increasingly slower, she also added a little trick of being an imbecile as well. Any Gestapo official would have given up in despair, impatient to get rid of her.

Stacey passed all tests with honours. She was learning all she could. At the same time, she did not neglect her nursing duties to her patient, Hans. She had to get him onto his feet, as quickly as possible; she had strict instructions from Captain Anderson to this effect.

Hans Olsen, her Swedish patient, obeyed her implicitly. He liked the bossy lady with her good sense of humour and kindness, and most of all, he admired her courage. She had saved his life, after all. Being in such close contact with her, Hans began to look for her and to rely on her. Every day she massaged his legs, bringing back the circulation, encouraging him to exert himself by moving from one chair to another. She managed to get him to move his legs within a day or two, also she taught him to take deep breaths, whilst performing the movement.

Her good organising abilities helped towards the smooth running of the group. Within days she had the kitchen organised giving Georges a daily routine of different menus. He loved her teamaking, which she made for him, and the other men. No one seemed to understand the easy machination of tea making, so Stacey was voted honourable tea maker by all the men. She forbade all callers, taking possession of the kitchen whilst feeding Hans herself, plus a strange brew of tea made up to a recipe of her own, which made him stronger.

In so doing, she made an enemy, unwittingly, of the young woman she had first seen, previously, crying in a corner before the appendicitis operation. The girl Jacqueline Moulin had prepared some delicacies of her own for the invalid. As she proceeded to take the tray in to Hans, she was stopped at the door by Stacey, who took the tray firmly out of her hands. 'Non, you are not allowed to visit the patient,' said Stacey, in her school girl French. Jacqueline glared at her, with hatred and resentment in her eyes, turning away without a word.

Chapter Eleven

There was no doubt that Stacey was attracted to this big, amiable Swedish giant, and he delighted in her attention. They would be forever exchanging stories, sometimes intimate stories of the past.

'You know, Hans,' Stacey once said to him, 'You may have wondered why I remained a 'miss' all my life and a regular in the Army for thirty years. You see, I loved once, only once, when I was twenty three. The man I fell head over heels in love with was ten years older than me, and married. He didn't hide the fact, although I felt it could come only to nothing, but I continued on this dizzy path of no return, I simply could not stop myself. We had many clandestine meetings, wonderful heady meetings. But, you know, what brought it to conclusion was his wife.' Stacey paused, then went on, 'She attempted suicide. As far as I was concerned, that finalised the whole affair, and brought me to my senses. I couldn't bring myself to be the reason of another's unhappiness, can you understand that?'

'Yes, of course,' Hans replied thoughtfully, 'were you a nurse, at the time?'

Stacey nodded.

'Well, that would make your reason even more of consequence.'

Stacey stared unseeingly at her hands, so she said simply, 'I have remained Miss Scott all my life.'

On other occasions Hans would inform her of details of his own life as a lumberjack, before the war, the open air life of his beloved Sweden. 'The life of a city dweller was not for me,' he said. 'My ambition was to become a forest surveyor, to preserve the trees and undergrowth in the woods and forests, against elm disease, and arsonists. My training was long and arduous, but after taking final exams, I decided to go to the main cities of the world, to obtain knowledge from professionals of the field, beginning in Paris. Instead of which I became swept up in your war, not even my war, being a neutral country, as you know.' He paused. 'When the occupation of the Germans in Paris occurred, I joined a Swedish organisation in helping Jewish and other nationalities escape from being deported to German Labour camps, hiding people in safe houses. In this way I was introduced to Combat, but, my dearest Stacey, if this situation had not happened I would not be holding your hands in mine.' His large hands, covered with golden hair, held her tiny hands in his grasp, they stayed in this stance for some considerable time.

Stacey kept her work in the kitchen only for Hans, and left the cooking for the men to Jacqueline and other women Resistance agents. This caused further friction between the two women, with Jacqueline going to Captain Anderson complaining that Stacey refused to work only for Hans, and was above putting herself out for anyone else. Jacqueline made it clear that she was happy cooking for the men, but she would not prepare food for Stacey. This was ignored by Captain Anderson, 'You will do what you are told' was the gruff reply.

After a few days, Stacey was sitting, waiting for lunch with the men, when the door burst open and Hans stood there, wobbling on his legs, with a bottle in one hand.

He roared 'Back on duty, sir' to Captain Anderson, and putting his arm affectionately round the shoulders of Stacey, he continued, 'This sir, is ma petite soldat. With permission, sir, I would like this to be her code name for London and for us.'

They all assented, springing onto their feet, toasting her 'our petite soldat' they chorused. Stacey was very happy. 'For ever,' she replied, raising her glass to them 'United we stand, until death us do part.'

But, the gesture of Hans did not go unnoticed by Jacqueline. She poured her wine, deliberately, on the floor, and walked out. Some time later, Stacey went to attend her patient; her hand was about to knock on the door, when she paused, her hand in mid-air. She was under discussion by Jacqueline and Hans. Sometimes the voices were low, other times, loud and heated. They were arguing in French, but she knew enough French to understand what was being said.

'She is old and ugly, what can you see in her? You are not to speak to her again. She must be told we are lovers,' the girl shouted at him.

Stacey went back to the table, she glanced swiftly at the men, but they avoided her eyes, pretending they did not hear the screaming row between the two. She heard Hans roar with laughter, he couldn't be bothered with this feminine jealousy, and he couldn't understand it. The more he laughed the angrier Jacqueline became but eventually their voices began to be subdued. They re-entered the room, Jacqueline was smiling as she shot a triumphant look at Stacey, her arm loosely curled round the waist of Hans.

From that moment on, Jacqueline made no attempt to hide her hostility to Stacey, but, as the bitter rivalry over Hans continued, it began to cause disorder amongst the other Resistance fighters, leaving Captain Anderson no alternative but to part them, having heard the many dissatisfied complaints about the two women.

Stacey became a letter box courier. Picking up messages in secret places, delivering them and passing further messages to Captain Anderson. Throughout these procedures, she never spoke, and was not accosted or assailed. Stacey would often think up ideas of her own, for passive sabotage, which would not have earned the approval of Captain Anderson. Her chief object was the railway. She discovered that their present position lay on the outskirts of Paris, in the woods near Versailles. She entered into Paris heading for the station 'Gare de L'East' on foot. The station was thick with troops carrying arms. At that time, throughout France, able bodied men and boys were called up to fight on the German front. Sudden round-ups and sweeps through towns and villages appalled the French nation, but they were helpless to object in any way. No one noticed a shrouded figure monkeying with the labels on trunks, so that German soldiers would find themselves with winter underwear, when they were expecting guns. On the same occasion, it so happened, a train was scheduled to leave for the German front, carrying so called French relief workers. A ceremony was under way, with brass bands and speeches. A whistle blew, the engine slowly puffed away, but the carriages remained obstinately on the platform. Who had uncoupled the carriages? The Germans looked at each other in bewilderment. The shrouded figure disappeared like a ghost.

Stacey became more proficient on each occasion. Hans took her with him on his dangerous sabotage activities. Disrupting railway lines, blowing up trains etc. They were always together, and not surprisingly they fell in love. To them, the situation was like a game. They never thought of their own safety. It was not only sabotage, though. Their unit was very short of cash, clothes and arms, so like shadowy thieves, they went out into the Paris streets, stealing, robbing, quite often with violence. Stacey would stand guard at a street corner, whilst Hans would relieve the erstwhile victim of his money. Any resistance, a quick blow would knock him out. All this would be done just before curfew at night, when people would be hurrying back to their dwellings, to beat the prohibition of being out of doors during specified hours.

There were times when they had to risk this escapade in the day. It is a rumoured fact that the richer classes in occupied France did little or nothing to help the Resistance cause. Another trick was to join food queues. Stacey was often sent out on this mission; mingling with hungry crowds was easy game. Purses, wallets and food cards, were her aim. She seldom returned with empty hands.

The Resistance fighters were desperately short of cash. Captain Anderson divided them into two groups, one group to raid a Bank, the other group to raid hospital supplies. The two women were divided as usual. Stacey was sent on the Bank robbery, and Jacqueline to rob medical supplies. They left their hideout at night, getting to Paris at early sunrise.

The plan was to use bicycles; the Parisians were all using bicycles as transport, so this type of travel was perfect for riding to the Bank, plus a getaway car after the raid, to pick them up outside the Bank.

They managed to find an old Citroen, making energy with a mixture of pig and chicken manure. The car was hidden in a garage, near to the Bank of their choice, to be brought out at a given time. Georges and his two comrades, Stacey and Hans, Luc and Jean were chosen for the raid. Stacey was dressed as a man with shaven head; a few sticks of dynamite were hidden inside her waistcoat, in case of real trouble. They all carried knapsacks. They synchronised watches for 11 a.m. They planned to enter the Bank quietly and go about their business in orderly efficiency, no shouting or frightening people. This they did at exactly 11 a.m. They split up, Stacey kept by the door, Jean and Luc covered the left hand side of the door, and the far side of the Bank. Hans sidled over to the French security guard, pushing a gun into his side. 'Put your hands behind your back, and you won't get hurt,' he hissed. With his foot, he pulled a chair behind the guard, and pushed him down onto it, manacling his hands to the back of the chair. At the same time, he gagged him. Stacey slipped a 'closed' notice on the door. Georges calmly made his way to the cashier's desk. He introduced himself with a smile, and politely pointed a gun at the cashier, the gun was covered by a large handkerchief.

Hans turned from the guard to the customers queuing behind Georges, covering them with his gun. They were unaware that the guard had been muffled. They gaped at Hans, as if he had come from outer space. 'We are Resistance fighters,' he said briefly, 'No tricks, behave quietly and normally and you won't get hurt. Cause a disturbance and you die instantly.'

All customers were individually frisked. Wallets, handbags, jewellery were taken roughly, and thrown into one of the rucksacks. Stacey took over from Hans, bringing out a stick of dynamite menacingly, leaving him free to help the others. In the meantime, Georges was demanding cash from the three cashiers.

'Now,' he ordered, pointing his gun at them. With the two desperadoes Luc and Jean, helped by Hans, they opened their knapsacks to receive the bundles of notes, as it was handed over to them from the tills. They did not want bloodshed, or the noise of flying bullets, which would attract attention from outside. Everything was to go smoothly and easily, as they had rehearsed beforehand, over and over again.

One bespectacled customer, who had protested loudly throughout, in spite of death warnings, proclaimed reasonably, 'Tous les clients sont du cote des combattants de la Resistance; il n'est pas besoin de nous maltraiter. D'ailleurs, nous voulons les aider autant que possible.'

'All the customers were on the side of the Resistance fighters, they did not need to be roughly used; in fact, they would give them all the aid they could possibly want.'

With that remark, Hans allowed the customers to turn round to face him, but no moving. The same procedure was obvious, in the way the cashiers avidly pushed as much cash into their eager hands.

At this point the Manager came out, his arms clasped round a bag of money. 'For the Resistance fighters' he said simply. Hans, the leader, bowed and thanked him profusely. After such hospitality, he felt obliged to release the security guard immediately. He made a little speech, 'Mesdames et Messieurs, priez de nous excuser de nos manieres quelque peu brutales. De meme, bien sur, a Mr le Directeur de cette Banque ainsi qu'a ses employes; nous regrettons de causer une telle interruption desagreable dans l'ordre de votre jour de travail mais notre devoir reste-et ceci parmi tous les Francais-de soutenir la Resistance. Vos offres ont de la valeur certainement mais surtout il nous faut etre rapides au-dessus de tout si l'on veut battre les possede, en particulier nos femmes, devenues maintenant vulnerables et sans protection aucune de cet adversaire immonde et vicieux. Joignez-nous dans notre combat pour la liberte.'

'Ladies and gentlemen, we apologise if you consider you have been roughed up, also to the Manager and his employees for the interruption of the smooth running of their Bank, but, it is the duty of all French people to aid the Resistance, we prize your offerings, but speed is essential for outwitting the Boche, who have invaded and raped our country of all it possesses; particularly our women, who are now vulnerable, unprotected from this vicious enemy. Join us in our fight for freedom.'

This speech brought a round of applause. The fighters were congratulated, everyone wanted to shake them by the hand, slap them on the back. This prompted the Bank Manager to bring out bottles of wine. He had waited all his life for this moment, when customers and the Bank were at one accord. The cashiers handed round glasses of wine, but Georges was getting impatient and anxious. It was all very well this bonhomie, but any of these people could betray them. The cashiers, the Bank Manager only had to press a bell, and the whole of Paris would be on the alert; not only that, their description would be given away, although they wore balaclavas. The whole incident by now, must have taken 30 minutes, whereas 10 minutes was the time allotted. He looked contemptuously at Hans and Stacey. How typical of them, what amateurs. His life was at stake, and the lives of the other freedom fighters, because of two foreigners, who considered the procedure as a game.

'For God's sake,' he screamed at them, 'grab the loot and get out.' It certainly brought them to their senses. Hans immediately became authoritative. They had their instructions.

The doors were opened, and with bulging knapsacks over their backs, they looked like any French farmer or worker, slipping unobtrusively into the background.

They had agreed previously only to use the car in dire circumstances; they were aware that the driver would watch their movements anxiously, until their safety was ensured. Quietly like ghosts, without hurrying, without any undue nervousness, they strolled to their bicycles, unlocked them, and pedalled away, mingling with the public.

Hans and Stacey were the last to leave, now keen to get away from the over attention of the Bank Manager, who seemed loath to let them go. It was at this moment that two Nazi Officers came into the Bank. The Bank Manager dropped the freedom fighters like hot cakes and scuttled back to his office. The whole situation had reversed, whereby before, patriotism and friendliness abounded, now people were afraid for their lives.

They shouted at the Officers, 'We have been robbed,' pointing accusing fingers at Hans and Stacey. 'Catch the thieves.' At the same time, the Security Guard placed himself in front of their only exit, pointing his machine gun at them. The Nazis were taken by surprise. 'You are both under arrest, drop your guns.'

Stacey screamed 'Dynamite,' at the same time, she threw the dynamite towards the Germans, where it lay at their feet, she dropped to the ground, cowering in a corner. This action distracted the Security Guard momentarily and the Nazi Officers. They were at a loss to know what to do, whether to throw themselves flat on the floor, or to shoot and ask questions afterwards, but their hesitation proved their undoing. Hans grabbed his automatic, shot the Security Guard, shot the two

Nazi Officers, both too slow to seize their pistols in time.

Hans and Stacey fled out of the place, and ran for their lives. They saw the Citroen waiting for them; Hans opened the back door, pulling Stacey in with him, but, within a second, he realised his mistake. It was the wrong car. In the back of the car sat a high ranking Nazi Officer.

'Merd' Hans gasped, flying headlong through the car, out of the back right hand door, with Stacey following. Then their luck ran out. Although Hans had overcome his astonishment, instantly, at finding a Nazi Officer in his, so he thought, get away car; the Officer had just as quickly overcome his astonishment in finding two people, presumably on the run, invading his private automobile. He leapt out after them. He managed to grab Stacey, levelling his army pistol at her head. He ordered Hans to drop his gun. Hans had no alternative but to obey.

'Put your hands on the car and spread your legs,' he rasped, throwing Stacey against the car at the same time. With dazzling speed, French and German Police came from all directions. Stacey felt rough hands searching her body thoroughly, they were surrounded, there was no way out. Satisfied that the prisoners had been handed over to military security, the German Officer climbed back into his car, and was driven away.

The French Police were often worse than the Germans in their bid to do their duty. The prisoners, with their hands manacled in front of them, were ordered to stand against a wall, with their hands above their heads, their legs spreadeagled. It was lunch time, and the French, due to tradition, dropped everything, and immediately the interest in the prisoners waned. For the French, (as had been so for centuries) food was their one and only concern, from twelve noon, to two p.m. Anything else was set aside, as of less importance. Stacey and Hans were left, guarded by two soldiers, with machine guns at the ready.

Hans turned to Staccy, 'If I never see you again, I love you Stacey.'

Stacey's eyes filled with tears, 'I love you,' she whispered.

Hans then turned to the young soldiers guarding him, 'Donne-moi une cigarette s'il te plait?' One soldier duly agreed, lighting the cigarette himself, then passing it to Hans, pushing it between his teeth. Hans puffed at it for a few minutes thoughtfully; he whispered to Stacey 'When I say run, run for it, don't follow me, split up.'

He turned again to his French guards, 'Qu'est-ce que vous foutez, travailler pour les Allemands? N'etes-vous pas donc Francais? Quand on gagnera cette guerre, on vous retournera en tant que traites de votre pays.'

'What the hell are you doing working for the Germans? Aren't you French men? When this war is won by us, you will be turned over as traitors to your country!'

The one soldier looked down uneasily. 'La ferme!' he snapped, but Hans did not give in. 'Pourquoi les aider, ils sont vos enemis. Vous vous mettez contre votre propre peuple; nous nous battons pour vous aider a vous debarrasser d'eux, hors de ce pays pour toujours.'

'Why help them,' he went on remorselessly, 'they are your enemies, you are turning against your own people, we are fighting to help you get rid of them, out of this country for ever!'

They spoke in undertones, apart from the anger of the guards, which erupted, now and then.

'Je dois obeir a mon devoir sinon je finirai moi aussi dans un camp de concentration.'

'I have to do my duty, otherwise I shall be in a concentration camp myself.'

Hans knew he had been brainwashed, but there was an unsureness about his words and manner, which enabled Hans to persist, and outline his plan to him. 'Laissez-nous partir, tu ne le regretteras pas. Je te cognerai, nous nous echapperons, puis tu tireras a l'air.'

'Let us go,' he begged, 'You won't regret it. I will knock you down, we will make a run for it, then you shoot into the air.' He knew he was taking an immense risk, the guard might shoot them anyway; he was also putting Stacey's life at risk, but nothing would stop him now; what had they to lose, whether the Gestapo killed them, or the guards. No member of the Resistance expected or received anything but the worst, including all who helped them, but if his plan was executed properly, they could all escape, including the guards.

The boy was on his side now. 'Frappe-moi dur. Mon pote ici vous tirera dessus mais il vous manquera. Si tu m'assommes comme il faut, ils sorest plus convinces par mon hipster.'

'Hit me, make it hard,' he said. 'My friend here,' alluding to the other guard, 'will shoot at you, but we will miss you,' he added excitedly. 'If you knock me out, they are more likely to believe my story.'

It was Hans who had to admit to the bravery of the guards. 'Donnez-moi vos noms et je vous recommenderai quand tout sera fini.'

'Give me your name, and I will recommend you, when this madness is over.'

The two soldiers gave their names, Hans memorised them. 'Le moment que je jette ma cigarette sera votre signal.'

'When I throw away my cigarette, that will be your signal.'

The boy did not answer, but looked furtively around, then pushed Hans against the wall roughly, adding a few swear words for good measure, then regained his position a few feet away, pointing his gun firmly at the head of Hans, after muttering a few words to his colleague. It was now or never.

Hans lowered his manacled hands from his head, with both hands, he threw away his cigarette, then turned on his custodian. With a quick blow he knocked the soldier out, only to be met with a hail of bullets from the remaining soldier.

'Run' he screamed at Stacey, whereupon they both flew in different directions. Twice, Stacey stumbled and fell, her hands, and wrists were bleeding from the manacles which bit into her flesh; covered with dust, she ran into streets, devoid of people. They were either at lunch, or found it safer to stay behind closed doors. On and on she ran.

Suddenly, she saw ahead of her, a crowd of people being searched by the police. They must have discovered her escape, she thought. Trembling with fright, her limbs scarcely co-ordinating, she stopped, turning down another street. The usual procedure of the Police was to block all roads.

Stacey saw a man standing on the opposite side of the road. With her manacled hands in front of her, she took off her cap, went up to the man and whispered 'Help me, don't give me away, they will kill me.' She reached up and took off his trilby, and put it on her head, and quietly strolled away. The man, understanding the situation, took her cap in exchange and placed it on his own head.

What the police saw were two men, walking in different directions. They decided to chase after the man with a cap on his head, as this was the description of Stacey which they sought, enabling Stacey to disappear into the shadows again.

Stacey walked the long way back to her base, on the outskirts of Paris, keeping to the side streets. What a sight she must look, she thought, covered with blood and dust, with her manacled hands in front of her, as if in prayer. She slipped quietly into the woods, furtively looking round, as she neared her destination. Was her imagination playing her tricks, or did there seem to be more troop activity than usual? She was so weary she could hardly draw one step after another, which made her less cautious, less aware of her own danger.

She heard the click of a gun, as she stepped into the arena of trees at the entrance of their refuge.

Luc, on sentry duty, barred her way. He had not immediately recognised her. She whispered the password. Seeing the state of her exhaustion, he slipped his arm round her and helped her into the mouth, which formed the gap of the torn down tree, their place of concealment, their hideout. Stacey was instantly surrounded by the Resistance fighters, asking all manner of questions. Hans was there, she noted with relief, with his big arms outstretched, hugging her, like a bear.

'Ma petite soldat,' he exclaimed proudly. They sat her down, and with a few deft strokes, they cut off the manacles. Hans took the cut and bleeding wrists, gently bathing them. It was obvious he loved her, his big hands were never clumsy. This giant of a man, who could, with one blow, kill another, tended her like a child, which aroused a longing in her, which could not go unanswered, and which she could not explain. Drawing her to her feet, he put his arm around her protectively, they then went to report to Captain Anderson, like two happy children.

Jacqueline, however, did not go unnoticed by Stacey. She was hovering in the background, there was venom and hatred in the whole stance of her face and body.

The reception they received from Captain Anderson was not what they expected. He was livid and oblivious to the discomfiture they had already received in the hands of the enemy. He put them on the carpet in no uncertain terms. 'I am extremely angry with you.'

When confronted by a furious Captain Anderson, the erstwhile culprit shrivelled into a nothing. When he did not shout, was when he was to be most feared. His voice was like a knifeblade, that struck into the victim like ice.

Stacey and Hans looked at each other in consternation. They had expected a rapturous reception from their leader, with congratulations from all and sundry, having pulled off a financial coup, without bloodshed.

'You were lucky to have got away with your lives, apart from putting the lives of your partners at risk. You were given precise timing at the Bank, ten minutes, instead of which, you turned the whole exercise into a farce, a jamboree. In so doing, you have brought the whole German army on our heads. They would have ground our whereabouts out of you, and blown you away, like the idiots you are.' He could hardly speak, he was so angry. 'This is war, not a game of Russian roulette. I am disappointed and disgusted with both of you. Dismiss.'

Stacey attempted to explain, but she was waved away with a flick of his hand.

'I have nothing more to say,' he turned his back on them, then, as an afterthought, 'Where is the money that should have been collected from the Bank by you? Back in the Bank vaults by now, no doubt.'

Stacey and Hans stared at the ground, shuffling their feet, shamefacedly. Stacey looked at Hans, and with a small shrug, they retired to the door. Whether Captain Anderson caught sight of this insolence, she never knew, but he reprimanded them again. 'Where do you think you are,' he barked, 'at a holiday camp? You salute a superior officer.'

They sprang to attention immediately, and saluted.

'Scott, you remain here; you can go.' He refused any further hearing from Hans.

With no preamble, he came straight to the point. 'A woman has been brought in, she has been thoroughly interrogated and cross examined by us, and is our prisoner. We believe her to be an Irish quisling, pretending to be a nurse. She is to be executed in the morning, first thing, by gunshot. You are to perform this duty, and that is an order. You are on your honour, not to discuss this with anyone.'

Stacey knew he was testing her, but she said nothing, but stared stoically ahead. 'You will report for duty at 600 hours,' he added.

'Sir' she saluted smartly, turned on her heel and left the room. She could never obey this order, he must know that, she thought; maybe she could faint at the final moment, or get a mysterious bug, that exempted her from duty; she considered all these excuses wildly. He would only have contempt for her. There was a perverseness in her character, which made her resist his exaggerated patriotism, but she was under his command, there was little she could do.

The next morning at precisely 600 hours, she reported to him. Captain Anderson was ready and waiting for her. With his usual icy precision, he took a small revolver from his desk drawer and handed it to her.

' Follow me,' he ordered curtly. She followed him into a small room devoid of furniture, in the middle of which stood a chair, with a woman sitting tied to the chair, with a cloth over her head. The woman was sobbing.

'I cannot do this, I am a nurse,' stuttered Stacey, 'this is plain bloody murder.'

'This is war,' was the steely answer. Stacey looked into his eyes, and realised he meant it. She turned on him 'You're a sadistic bastard.' She went over to the woman, and before she could be stopped, she had whipped off the hood, and cradled the woman's head in her arms. Then, she stepped back in astonishment as she recognised Teresa.

Captain Anderson drawing his service revolver strode over to the two women. 'Orderly,' he shouted, 'this woman,' indicating Stacey 'is on a charge of treason. Take her away.'

But Stacey interrupted him, 'This woman, sir, is Teresa O'Conner, trainee nurse, now a Sister at the British Military Hospital of the 11th Casualty Clearing station in Abbeville, France. She was a close friend of mine, we trained together. I beg you, sir, to at least hear her out and then make your decision.'

There was a silence. Captain Anderson stood for a moment, undecided, then grabbing a chair and placing it in front of him, he sat astride the chair, his gaze never leaving the two women. 'Right' he said, his eyes glittering behind his pince-nez, 'We will get to the bottom of this, and it had better be good.'

Stacey turned to the sobbing Teresa taking her face in her hands. 'Don't cry, kid' a special word she had always called Teresa. 'Take your time,' and gently she took the shaking hands. 'Tell Captain Anderson and me, what happened to you on that terrible day…I should never have left you…but what was I to do?'

'Orderly,' shouted Captain Anderson, 'Tea for the ladies. Now.' He always felt at a loss with women, men, he could order about as much as he liked, but with women, he felt he was on a losing battle, never the victor.

When tea arrived, there was clearly a relaxation in the room. Teresa hugged and kissed Stacey, mopping her eyes with the handkerchief handed to her by Captain Anderson. Stacey, all the time stroking Teresa's hair, sat beside her, giving her the courage to tell her story, and slowly, stumbling, Teresa began to tell her story. She began softly, gaining confidence as she proceeded…

Chapter Twelve

Teresa's story

In her soft Irish brogue, she unfolded her story…'I stayed, three hours or thereabouts, under that bed in the hospital. The Gestapo had taken Rachel away, and had long since gone, I was very frightened. The hospital ward became darker, before I dared to emerge; Sergeant Thompson and the medical orderly lay where they had been struck down. I did not dare to look at them, lying silently on the floor in pools of blood. I didn't know what to do. Rachel's husband, Joseph, lay staring at the ceiling. I remember going over to him, and closing his eyes. The four other patients lay in grotesque attitudes, enclosed by sheets, which looked like white ghosts in the moonlight. I remember walking towards the orderly room, with the purpose of finding something to eat and drink. I must have wandered about the hospital for three days, when I heard cars and men's voices. I had already found a place of concealment, far less conspicuous than under the bed, so I hid in this cupboard, until they had all gone.'

'This story is ridiculous,' said Captain Anderson, 'I think you're lying, to save yourself.'

'Oh please, Captain Anderson hear her out,' pleaded Stacey. Teresa took no notice, she was in her own world of remembrance.

'The Germans had removed the bodies, padlocking the doors. There were enough provisions to keep me going, and I stayed aimlessly, too terrified to leave and too scared to stay. My indecision made me lethargic; a lot of the time I stayed in one of the beds, sleeping or just staring up at the ceiling, going over and over again in my mind, the terror of what I had seen happening to my only friends.' Teresa paused, she looked past Stacey and Captain Anderson, as if they were not there. She continued 'At the same time, the longer I remained, the deeper my danger, what if they came back, or transferred the hospital to an army unit for their own troops? It was unlikely they would just leave the hospital, as it was. All these thoughts crossed and recrossed my mind, also the food was running out. I decided to leave that night, as soon as it was dark enough. I filled my sleeping bag, with as much food as I could carry, and strapped it over my back. In my possessions, I had a jumper, which partly hid my uniform, I also took my nurse's cape for warmth at night. The trouble was I had no money, no credentials, only Sergeant Thompson's teachings of how to defend myself. I did have, however, a gold cross given to me at my christening, I wore this round my neck. I found a small lethal kitchen knife, which I strapped to my leg.'

Stacey and Captain Anderson listened intently; Teresa looked at them but did not see them. 'There was a full moon that night, and the country surrounding the hospital looked like daylight, but I was determined to leave. I smashed a hole in the downstairs window to enable me to escape. I could never have managed the padlocked doors. I ran to the gates of the hospital, which were also locked, scaled the enclosure wall by climbing a very unsteady tree, and slipped into the woods nearby. A path had been cut in the woods, and I followed it. I thought, I could find my way to Paris, so kept on a southern course, relying completely on the small compass I had in my possession, as taught by Sergeant Thompson. I did my travelling by night, and slept as well as I could by day. Time no longer had any interest for me, but I kept walking, I must have covered several miles.' Teresa paused again, taking a sip of tea before continuing. 'On the whole, as it was summer time, my daytime sleeping arrangements went very well; I kept well to the trees, always covering myself with foliage, freshly cut each day, with my knife, for concealment. At dusk, I made a small fire with twigs, and feasted on the food I had obtained from the hospital, but I longed for a good meal and ached from the continuous rain. I kept to small roads and paths, keeping well out of sight I must have skirted many towns and villages, but by the third day my food ran out, and I was famished by hunger and thirst.'

'This Sergeant Thompson certainly knew how to train you and Sister Scott, a man after my own heart I would say,' said Captain Anderson. Stacey looked at him, he was becoming immersed in Teresa's story; also, it was the first time she had ever heard him complimenting her.

'He taught us how to defend ourselves,' said Teresa simply.

'Carry on,' said Captain Anderson impatiently.

'Well, I was determined that at the next farm I came to, I would have to steal. Eggs, milk, whatever I could find. Scruples I had about stealing, had long been forgotten; all I was interested in, was to keep my strength to survive. If I faltered at all, I would be lost. I had lived on a farm, with my parents in County Wicklow, and I was very used to farm life, it was second nature to me. I had struggled to the top of a wooded slope. Below me, I could see from afar, in the valley, a few shops, a little church, and, on the outskirts I spotted a farm. I must admit I longed to be part of that community, it seemed so peaceful…' Teresa sighed, as she remembered the tranquility of the scene. 'By nightfall, I carefully circled the district, waiting for people to return to their homes, securely locking and bolting their doors, before I dared to move, and make for the barn. The door creaked ominously, I felt sure it would wake the inhabitants of the house, but hunger pushed me on. I could hear the restless stirrings and chewing of the animals. I struck a match, and the cows turned and looked at me with their soulful eyes, still chewing. I was knowledgeable in milking cows, four a.m. was my usual morning routine, back at home,' Teresa said proudly. Stacey laughed. 'But, as I had no container, I bent down to the nearest animal and drank from her teat. I then searched the barn, for maybe further replenishment. I found a section that was used for storing, butter, cheese, eggs, tea, tobacco, everything that I could wish for, like an Aladdin's cave. I filled my nurse's cape with as much as I could manage, turning it into a knapsack by tying the edges together, in the middle. I picked up my so called swag, preparing to depart in haste, when I heard a distinct click of a gun. I froze where I stood, not daring to move. In the gloom, I saw the outline of a woman, carrying a double barrelled shotgun, which was levelled straight at my head, at the same time a nonstop flow of French proceeded from her. I did not speak. Eventually, she signalled me, to follow her into the house. Still keeping me within the sights of her gun, she bent down to telephone. I presumed the Police. This action had an immediate effect on me, I sprang forward 'Non' which triggered off a blast from her shotgun, most of which went into her ceiling, thank goodness. I dived behind the sofa, I thought she was the Devil Incarnate, and crossed myself many times, I would have included a 'Hail Mary' instead of which from that unsafe position, I gabbled out a mixture of French and English, mostly English, that I was Irish, a neutral country. I would do anything she wanted, but please do not call the Police. The woman lowered the gun, and a crafty expression came over her face. 'Engleesh, eh!' 'No, Irish.' I hesitated to correct her. 'All the same,' and a further volley of abusive French followed.'

Captain Anderson and Stacey both roared with laughter at her story. 'Go on, this is really funny,' they said.

'I didn't understand what was said,' continued Teresa, 'but I imagined we were the cause of the war. 'I am tired and hungry,' I interrupted, 'Work first, eat after' was my brisk reply. The kitchen was untidy, dirty, but I was only too willing to comply. I washed up, scrubbed the floor, tidied as well as I could, with the woman standing over me all the time, still training the gun at my head, all this in the middle of the night. 'Come' she ordered, taking an oil lamp, I followed her into a loft,

'Sleep.' I unrolled my sleeping bag. She brought me a stew of sorts, plus a hunk of bread. I was so tired, I fell asleep in the middle of eating. It seemed, I had not been asleep for five minutes, when I was roughly awakened by the woman. 'Work' she insisted, 'the cows, milk.' Although I could speak little French, it was easy to understand her. In a half stupor, with my eyes practically closed, I followed her down to the same barn, as before. She seated me on a bucket, whilst systematically I milked twenty cows, then came the hen house, which had to be cleaned, the eggs collected, and all this at 4 a.m. in the morning. She rewarded me with a plate of gruel, ham, eggs, and a mug of coffee; my respite was short lived however, as a pile of washing was produced from nowhere, and the whole pattern of work started again. By the time I had cleaned out every room, made the beds, washed up at breakfast, ironed the clothes, prepared the vegetables for the small bistro run by Madame, washed up the lunch, sparkled the glasses from the bar, it was five p.m. and a whole basket of sewing was again found from nowhere. Madame Bisset, for that was the woman's name, was a harridan of the worst kind. She harassed and bullied me all day long, but, as in all things, I became used to this bombardment, and found all ways and means of escaping her. I began to think, maybe there was a possibility of staying, till the duration of the war, snug and safe in the attic. Surprisingly enough, in the long run, I became quite fond of Madame Bisset. I could not forget, although she pushed my patience to the extreme, by pestering me endlessly, that she was risking her life in housing me, and because of this, I was forever in her debt. From what I gathered with gesticulation and nonstop flow of French, she had lost her son, almost on the outbreak of war, in the first few skirmishes for power. Sometimes, I would find her gazing at me, with a great sadness in her eyes, and I would try to distract her attention, onto something else, I could not bear her looking at me, with her eyes full of tears.'

Teresa paused, now there was a deep silence in the room, a pin could have dropped, Stacey and Captain Anderson would not have heard it. Teresa resumed her story, 'As time went on, I became bored, bored and restless, being confined to a house and an attic, is not funny. Two or three months passed, and my restlessness and boredom increased. One day I decided to take a chance, just by walking a few yards around the house perhaps…with success, came boldness.

Next day, I resolved to walk to the nearest town, or village, and just mingle with the people, anything that was different. I consoled myself with the idea that after an hour or two, I could slip back to my residence, unnoticed, or so I thought. If, I did nothing to expose myself, or draw attention to myself, my safety was assured. I walked into the suburbs of a town called Amiens. It was a market day, but there were few people and little to sell, on the few trestle tables, sparse vegetables, second hand clothes, etc; walking further into town, I was constantly on the alert for Wehrmacht patrols, and plainclothes men, as I had no identity papers on me, which would mean imprisonment, if caught, or worse. Here, there was more activity, the cafes were full of German military, their wives, sweethearts, or/and collaborators. A military band was playing, and in its wake, a military parade. Keeping well on the fringe, but intermingling with the small crowd which had collected to watch the proceedings, I noticed a group of Army Officers who were taking the salute, one of which, with sweat pouring down his face in the hot sun, was obviously in great discomfort. His discomfiture was ignored by the other Officers. They, with rigid stance, and arms pressed forward in the 'Heil Hitler' salute, were intent only in their duty. I thought to myself 'that man will fall in a moment'; this is exactly what happened, he slumped where he stood foaming at the mouth. No one moved, it was as if it had never happened. So what made me spring forward, with no regard to my own safety, I don't really know. The man was in a state of epilepsy, and was having an epileptic fit. I suppose the training I had had, the very fact that I was a nurse, trained to help in an emergency, made my action involuntary. Reflecting back on it, later, I thought I must be mad.'

'Mad,' spluttered Captain Anderson. 'Stupid more likely.'

Teresa coloured, she did not like being criticised, she tried to explain, 'My only instinct was to help this man, you must understand. I rushed forward, speaking incoherently in schoolgirl French, that I was a nurse. In front of all these dignitaries, I undid his collar, opened his jacket, and undid his belt. I snatched off my cardigan, made it into a kind of pillow, forcing the leather part of his belt into his mouth, which was shut like a clamp. Luckily the convulsions of his body slowly ceased, he opened his eyes, only once, I was not sure whether he knew what was happening or not; he looked straight at me, his eyes were an electrifying light blue, before sighing and lapsing into a trance like sleep. The Parade continued, as if this scene had never unfolded. I looked up suddenly, aware of my own danger, 'Il dorme,' I faltered, 'he must not be disturbed.' I considered, you may think naively, that the Germans were no better at speaking French than I was, but I quickly decided to make a hasty retreat. No one had seized me, or tried to prevent me, which was strange beyond a doubt, but I did not wait to find out. The Secret Police who were mingling with the crowd, had already espied me, and were converging upon me, I fled into the crowd. I began to realise my stupidity, when the French turned against me, as well as the Germans. In my thoughtlessness and impetuosity, I had helped one of their hated enemies, they would not forgive me for that, they would catch me and turn me over to the Police. Two or three of them barred my way, but I was quicker and nimbler, although they caught my clothing, they did not catch me. The Secret Police, not realising quite what was happening, began arresting my would-be pursuers, which saved my life. I plunged into the stalls, diving under the trestle tables, which were covered with check table cloths. The women, managing the stalls, were aware of my predicament, but not having seen the previous situation, were not antagonistic towards me. I put my finger to my lips, and with my heart thudding, I just prayed. In the position I was in under the tables, as you can imagine, I watched all kinds of boots…' This amused Stacey, who laughed out loud, they both laughed together, 'As they searched for me I heard the Police fire a number of questions at the women, but they answered with negative replies. I waited there, endlessly, until dusk had fallen and night had swiftly approached.

When it was safe, the women gave me the wink, shoving chocolate and French bread into my starving hands, they showed me the way back into the woods. I naturally, hurriedly resumed my way to Madame Bisset's house, but when I returned there, I gazed upon a horrendous scene. Madame Bisset was being bundled into a Gestapo car, the house was surrounded by Police. I could hear her voice imploring them; today, even it is implanted in my memory 'This nurse, what nurse? I do not know this nurse.' I was in a state of agitation, and great indecision, whether to give myself up, announce my Irish nationality, claim neutrality, but, it possibly would not necessitate the release of Madame Bisset. They would charge her for complicity, in hiding even a neutral person. Her duty being, that she should have immediately informed the Police of my presence, and because she had failed in her duty, she would get many years of imprisonment; on the other hand, if I kept quiet and said nothing, there was a good chance that she would be released out of lack of evidence. I must admit I did not want to tempt providence, and I soon persuaded myself, that I could make things worse by owning up. I decided to get out of the province as quickly as possible and strike again for the north of France, to the sea, in a forlorn hope that maybe there would be a ship or boat to take me back to England. With this in mind, keeping my compass in a north westerly direction, I started walking again, sleeping by day, and moving by night. It must have been about three days later, that your men Captain Anderson, picked me up and brought me here…' her voice trailed into silence. There was a hush in the room.

Captain Anderson stood up. 'Right,' he said, 'Teresa O'Conner stand up.'

Bewildered, Teresa and Stacey both stood. Turning to Stacey, he said, 'Scott, you will teach O'Conner all you know about being a Resistance fighter, good luck to you,' and as an afterthought, 'Your code name will be 'The Prisoner',' giving her one of his rare smiles, he shook Teresa by the hand and departed without looking round.

Stacey took Teresa's arm introducing her to the rest of the Resistance members. Stacey taught Teresa all she knew and more; she found Teresa a willing, enthusiastic pupil, with one drawback, her impetuosity.

Captain Anderson was well pleased with the results. There was little time to control her rash impulses, he considered she was too sensible to make silly mistakes, and decisions had to be made.

Teresa was given her first fairly simple task, of sending through letter boxes, miniature cardboard black coffins. French collaborators were a curse to the freedom fighters, undermining the fine work they were doing in freeing France from this vicious enemy. On the card would be printed the victim's name. Collaborators were to be executed, this was no mean threat, but reality, the sentence carried out, accordingly. There would be no mercy for collaborators.

It was dusk about 3 p.m. Nightfall came quickly at this time of the year in Paris 1941. It would be impossible to believe, that the muffled figure of peasant Teresa, staring back at her own photograph on so many buildings, was the same smiling nurse, with a reward of 10, 000 francs on her head. Anyone offering knowledge of her whereabouts to the Police, that is anyone brave enough to face the Gestapo.

Teresa furtively glanced round, her face momentarily caught in the moonlight. There was not a sound to be heard. Curfew was early, it was not wise for Parisians to be out on streets, in blacked out Paris. Teresa stepped out of the shadows. From the knapsack over her shoulders, she pulled a card, stopping every now and then, to slip a coffined card through various letter boxes. At one specific address, mingling with high ranking German officers, was a well known French informer. His name was on one of the cards. Teresa crept up to the door, attempting to slip the card under the door. From within, she heard the Germans singing national marching songs, the strains of 'Lily Marlene' accompanied with roars of raucous laughter. As she did so, the door was flung open by a German Officer, taking the Officer and her by surprise.

The Officer was the first to recover from his shock, demanding harshly her reasons for being there. Teresa dropped her cards and ran for it, dropping the knapsack as she went. She fled round the house into the garden. Suddenly, the curtain of darkness was pierced by a blinding light immediately in front of her. Again, another battery of lights were switched on behind her. She was caught.

The Estate was very large. At the end of the rose garden was a swimming pool, further on never ending hayfields, with a river lazily flowing towards a sea outlet. Dogs were given her knapsack to smell, and were unleashed. She sped in front of them, caught in a blaze of light. Teresa zigzagged from one side to the other, her eye catching a mound of manure left by some gardener. She threw herself on to it covering her legs up to her very thighs in the muck, in an effort to outmanoeuvre the dogs. She then rushed to the river, plunging into it, up to her neck in swirling waters, leaves and dead flowers. She could hear the barking of the dogs on the bank. Torches, lights of any kind, were used to pierce the gloom of the eddying waters, in search of her.

Often, Teresa had to keep her head under water, to escape her pursuers, taking great gulps of air to sustain herself. She waited until dawn, not daring to move. By this time, luckily, the Germans had tired of hunting their prey, and had withdrawn back to the house.

Shivering, wet, she emerged from the river, like a drowned rat, and hurried back to her sanctuary in the woods. Parisians, in those days, looked the other way when they were confronted by such a bedraggled object, or else informed the Police. They considered, in the most part, it was better to know little or nothing at all, certainly not to involve themselves, circumstantial to their surroundings. It was this she counted on. As it was, there were few people about, but what she had not counted on was the fact that the enemy had perfected their detection methods to such a considerable degree, that radioed messages could be traced within three and a half square miles. Paris had been cut into small squares, which were under constant check. Still keeping to the doorways, shooting into deserted streets and alley ways, she neared her destination on the outskirts of Paris, surrounded by woods.

Cutting deeply into the woods, Teresa approached their hideout, to be immediately challenged by Luc, she whispered 'Combat'. He stood aside, she entered the internal passage way, smiling.

She was met by Captain Anderson, with a curt command 'Get those wet clothes off, now.' He had hardly uttered his words, when there was an almighty crash, shaking the very foundations of their hideout. Captain Anderson glared at Teresa, 'You have allowed yourself to be followed, you fool.'

There was no time for further comment. Immediately, came organised chaos. All the Resistance had been trained into how to handle the situation of the discovery by the enemy of their cave. Papers, and all urgent documentation, were burnt instantly. The operators, with their signalling equipment, had to be protected, at all costs.

Captain Anderson took complete control, with his icy cool instructions, he gave the men the courage which had momentarily left the whole company. He seemed to be everywhere, in fact, a whole army, in one man. Encouraging here, shouting there, he put together quickly a trained force of Resistance men, ready for armed combat.

The Germans, with a whole army unit behind them, rushed their hideout with grenades. The Resistance, with admirable precision, picked up the grenades and hurled them back, at the same time, getting their one and only bazooka ready, to be fired by Georges. Next, the Germans tried lowering a bomb, on a string from above, but the Resistance cut the string, throwing the bomb back on the enemy.

The Germans did not attempt to come too near, but began machine gunning the entrance of their hideout. The Resistance began to make their exit, going backwards into the cave. Booby traps had been set at the mouth of the cave, should anyone be foolish enough to enter and follow them. Georges, with the help of Captain Anderson, timed their exits, so that the bazooka exploded the machine gun nests of their enemies.

It seemed to the Germans that the Resistance had more men and more ammunition than was originally supposed. The Germans attacked by propelling their flame throwers, sheets of flame caught the bracken and trees around the entrance. The men holding the flame throwers, walking bodily into the cave, were blown sky high by the booby traps.

By this time, the Resistance had dug themselves well into the cave, and were crawling along tunnels, just big enough for one man, or high enough for one man. They held soaked petrol rags, tightly wired, round sawn off branches, over their heads. The fighters had rehearsed this exit numerous times before, and knew exactly their own positions, and that of their comrades. Having tunnelled through a multitude of man made burrows, they emerged into the night air, many kilometres away.

They quickly made a break for freedom; luck was on their side, as the whole of Paris, outskirts included, was ensconced by thick mist. One by one, the men, like shadows of the night, slipped into Paris, and disappeared.

Chapter Thirteen

The Freedom Fighters

Stacey picked up her groceries, having joined long queues from early morning. Food was scarce, shelves were sparse, stores had little left, people queued for hours, only to be turned away. She hurried down various streets.

She had just slipped into the Rue des Anges when she saw a detection van, only a few yards away. She retreated back to whence she came, calculating another way of getting to her safe destination. She manoeuvred carefully to elude the van, until she came to a house on a corner dividing two streets. This house was known as a 'safe house'.

Stacey ran up the stone steps, once inside, she dashed up the staircase to a top room. The room was bare of essentials, apart from cooking utensils, enough room, however, for a radio transmitter receiving set. The room served as a transmitting area to London. Several of the Resistance fighters, working by day in local factories, lived in this dwelling, as a safe house. These houses had to be changed consistently for fear of German patrols, discovering, intercepting, and tracking down transmissions to London.

Stacey laid the bag of food on the table, and was greeted by Hans, who was alone. Hans carefully locked the two intercommunicating doors, then, enfolded her in his arms. In their passionate embrace, they were too concerned with each other to notice the handle of the first door being silently turned, in a secret effort to open the door. Stacey, eager to feel his lips on hers, impatiently with deft fingers undid buttons and zips that got in the way, until nakedness exposed their desire, for this brief moment of conjugal love.

On the hard parquet floor lay two cushions, enough support for her body, as he entered into her, easily and quickly, with sharp movements. She pushed her pelvis against him, to receive the full penetration, her excitement coming in little gasps, until she cried out involuntarily as he climaxed inside her. The two participants lay panting after their exertions, oblivious of the turning of the second door handle, as if some desperate person would gain entrance to their love making, however embarrassing…The tapping of a code message on the transmitter interrupted their dreams, bringing them back to reality.

At the same time, Luc, Teresa, Georges and Marc were agitatedly knocking at the door, they must leave at once.

Grabbing on clothes, they opened the doors, without a word, seizing the transmitter, radio equipment, they retreated through the loft exit, clambering onto the roof. Roof tops was a method, howbeit slow, of travelling sometimes for miles. Precariously they balanced onto roofs of different shapes and sizes, clinging to chimney pots, crawling along gutterings. From afar, they could see the detection van. They could neither proceed or recede from their positions, without being discovered. They must wait for the night.

At dusk, they moved their cramped bodies, wending their way to a further 'safe house'. This was a normal part of their lives. Safe houses were only safe for a few days, sometimes only for hours. The owners put themselves at considerable risk. The houses were used for radio transmission to London, and for concealment of the Resistance.

When, at last, they arrived at their destination, swinging down from the roof, they were greeted by Captain Anderson, relieved and pleased to see them, but keen and eager to hand them their next assignment. The elimination and execution of a French informer. As they listened to his plan, they felt warm and comfortable round a large table, provided by the lady of the house. Food and wine flowing, they again renewed their vows, devoting their lives to the freedom of Paris. They toasted each other and the landlady.

Stacey noted Jacqueline beside Captain Anderson, adhering to his every wish, jumping to attention when he snapped his fingers. Although she had ingratiated herself to his side, Stacey perceived he still treated her uncivilly, impatiently, irritably, in the usual Captain Anderson style.

After dinner, when they were rested, laughing at their ugly experiences, which fled before them like shadows in the night, as if they had never happened, Captain Anderson outlined his immediate plans. The elimination of a collaborator and informer, who had already sent many people to their death.

The man was a certain Jean de Laney, head porter of a well established block of flats, in the heart of Paris. He was an expert decorator, which enabled him to worm his way into the affairs of others, by repairing and painting their flats. People who could afford these luxuries were usually black marketeers, with fingers in many pies. When the occupants were not at home, he would systematically, carefully obtain any information he could find, and report his findings to the Police.

A known homosexual, he frequented the 'queer' bars. His particular vice, boys in their early teens, preferably with no money, no parental control. He was particularly fond of one boy, who he housed well away from where he worked. Every morning at nine a.m. he reported for work, and every evening at six p.m. he left for his love nest. Taking the Metro at George V, and alighting at Pont de Neuilly.

The Resistance had shadowed him for many weeks, he was a creature of habit, which was useful for them. They knew his every move. They reported back to Captain Anderson every detail of his accommodation, even down to the toys that were littered throughout his flat. He had received one of Teresa's black coffins, and asked for protection from the Police. The Resistance fighters would take him out, on his way home, as he stood awaiting the train, in the rush hour. No one would realise, until it was too late, that he had been quietly without fuss, eliminated by a push onto the electric line.

Stacey and Teresa were to be the 'look outs' to make sure the plan was successfully carried out, and if necessary to keep the police at bay, by shooting at their legs. They all knew their aversion to murder. Luc and Georges were drawn to be the assassinators. At five forty five p.m. they were at their specific places. The Metro was packed with workers going home. Stacey had a newspaper in her hand, and was steadily gazing at it, so it seemed. She had the advantage of being able to see the whole station, without raising suspicion. Teresa mixed with the crowd, her nose also buried in a newspaper.

The two Sisters watched De Laney as he sat on a seat, waiting for his train. The Resistance fighters slipping down next to him, on either side. They saw Luc speaking, his lips moving. De Laney let out a cry and leapt up. Then everything happened at once.

The Resistance forced him to the edge of the platform, but he was obviously putting up a fight. He yelled with all his might, the man was well built and strong. The train approached, the fighters had not wished to cause a furore by firing at him, only to neatly push him over the edge, onto the electric line, then a quick getaway; but De Laney clung to Georges.

The plan had gone badly wrong, not only was he knocking the daylight out of the slight Georges, but the noise alerted the Police. Within seconds, the Police, who were expecting their informant to be attacked, had emerged from the crowd to arrest the two Resistance fighters. At this moment in time, Stacey made her move, firing at the legs of the Policemen, which immobilised them; they collapsed, trampled under the feet of the crowd. The train entered the station with a roar. Teresa without pausing, threw her body at De Laney, who had just picked himself up from his fight with Georges, he was not expecting this hurtling body thrust at him, he lost his balance and fell onto the line. In desperation,

Teresa turned to the crowd round her with a cry 'Resistance! Aidons nous!'

The crowd parted and reclosed round the fighters, who just as quickly dropped their weapons, resuming their original disguises of farming peasants. The train stopped, a few yards away from the body on the line. Hooters blared, the station was cordoned off. The Germans were baffled, they organised a table at the entrance of the station, and through a tannoy, they ordered the station to be cleared, all identity papers to be produced. They were determined to weed out the assassins, no one would escape through their net.

Slowly the shuffling line stumbled forward, each person being carefully scrutinised. A few of them were picked out at random for questioning, with a strong possibility of punishment execution; but, surprisingly the fighters were bypassed without mishap.

They regrouped, some way from the station. They decided, between them, to phone through to their 'safe house'. Stacey rang giving the password, and received the correct answer from Jacqueline.

Stacey was surprised to hear Jacqueline's voice, as she had been given strict instructions from Captain Anderson never to answer the phone, in any circumstance.

'What's wrong?' asked Stacey suspiciously.

'Nothing is wrong,' the voice answered, smoothly and plausibly. 'Come quickly, we are waiting for you.'

Stacey was unsure, her instincts told her that something was wrong, and yet she had no means of knowing. 'O.K. We will be there in a minute,' she said putting down the receiver. She turned to Teresa, 'I think there is something wrong,' she said.

'Why?' Teresa queried.

'I don't know. Jacqueline answered the phone!'

Luc interrupted 'So what' was the enigmatic reply, 'We must report to the Captain, you know how impatient he gets, if he is kept waiting.'

With that, the four approached the house. There was nothing to be alarmed about, there was not a sound to be heard. They crept warily up the stairs. Stacey led the foursome, cautiously she opened the door.

To her astonished eye, she saw Jacqueline sitting on the table, swinging her legs, clad in silk, beautifully dressed, her hair coiled in the latest French fashion, glancing up and flirting with two strangers, a far cry from the peasant girl, sobbing in the corner when first discovered by Stacey.

Stacey opened her mouth to speak, then let out a cry; in the corner, in a grotesque bloodied heap lay her beloved Hans. The Resistance fighters leapt for the exit, but were surrounded. At the same time, the two strangers introduced themselves. SS, Obersturmfuhrer and Untersturmfuhrer, top Senior Officials.

Jacqueline jumped off the table when she saw Stacey, rapidly speaking in French, 'Tu pensais que tu pouvais me tromper, espece de salope, qu'est-ce que ton amant a de bon maintenant? Tu es a blamer, toi et tous les autres. Tu m'as traite comme un bon a rein. Tu n'as jamais apprecie ce que j'ai fait, meme ce que j'ai fait pour mon pays. Je peux le dire maintenant. Les Francais et les Anglais sont finis, les Allemands vont gagner la guerre. Donc qui a le dernier mot maintenant?'

'You thought you could deceive me, you bitch, what good is your lover now? You are to blame, you and all the others. You treated me as useless, as a nothing. You never appreciated what I did, or what I did for my country. I can say now. The French and English are finished, the Germans will win the war, so who is having the last laugh now!'

Her triumph was assured. Her revenge was complete. Hysterically she gave reasons for her betrayal, ticking them off, one by one on her fingers. The centre of all her accusations was Stacey, as she desperately searched for justification of her treachery.

Stacey stared at her, she was too stunned to speak, at last she said hoarsely 'I hope you are happy with your day's work. But don't think you will get away with it. This war will not last for ever; when the Germans are finished with you, they will kill you, if not, the French and British will condemn you.'

This brought a further barrage of invective. The old enemies faced each other with deadly hatred, it was to be a fight to the death. Knives were tossed to them, and grabbed ferociously by the well matched contestants. Luc and Teresa tried to interfere, but the strangers held them back. What did they care, if the two women killed each other. It would save them the task anyway, it was a spectacle, not to be missed, it appealed to their sadistic tendencies.

The two opponents crouched in the classic stance of the experienced knife fighter, circling round each other, like two bantam cockerels in an arena. They used every trick taught to them by the Resistance, forgetting they had both been taught in the same school.

Strange, how thoughts of no consequence came to Stacey, as they encompassed each other, carefully keeping out of arm's length. It will all be over in seconds, she thought, knives have no hesitation, a few slashes, and that's it. It is true, what they say, drowning people do see their lives flash in front of them. However hard she tried, she could not focus on the reality of the moment.

Jacqueline's knife slashed at her face. Stacey automatically went to defend the action, at the same time, with the swiftness of a snake, Jacqueline's knife came down, grazing the ribs, and into the abdomen, the death blow. Stacey felt the knife penetrate her abdomen like cold ice, turning she tried to speak, but could not, only a kind of gurgle escaped from her lips, as she slowly fell under the knife's pressure, as it tore at her guts.

She did not die immediately, as the life poured out of her, she observed the figures standing over her, as in a haze. She saw the fighters being rounded up, the small room filled with German soldiers. Stacey could see she had wounded Jacqueline badly, her arm was hanging loosely, and blood was pouring down her side. Eventually the room became silent. Stacey pulled herself over to where Hans's body was lying on the ground. She felt for his lifeless hand, and grasped it…

Down the stairs, the Resistance fighters were pushed, manacled together, Luc, Teresa, Georges, Marc, a bedraggled few, hardly recognisable as the proud heroic fighters they were, a few months ago. Silently, bitterly, they moved down the stairs, and into the waiting cars.

As she stepped into the car, Teresa let out a gasp, as she perceived the figure sitting upright in the back of the car. It was Captain Anderson, but what a different Captain Anderson. His eyes were slits, between two blackened bruises, his face swollen beyond recognition, his lips were split and blood was oozing from a gash in the forehead.

Teresa sat down beside him, in the back of the car; nothing was said, it was as if they had both turned into statues, as they stonily gazed out of the windows. The car swept through the snowbound streets, as Parisians apathetically shovelled snow into the gutters. Bread queues had formed in front of shop windows, windows, displaying their meagre ware. Teresa stared at them, as the car flew by. She felt she was another person, in another time.

The car reached its destination. The Gestapo headquarters at 82, Avenue Foch, Paris. The fugitives were thrust out of the car, and forcibly hustled up the steps.

As they reached the door, standing within this great hall, stood the same Nazi Officer she had helped to save, in an epileptic fit many months ago; Teresa let out an incredulous cry. He had recognised her, there was no doubt of that, the blue eyes swept over her, and rested on her own.

He looked as if he was going to speak, he stepped forward, 'One moment,' he said in German to her Police guard, as the Guard was about to propel the group forward.

She grasped her opportunity, speaking urgently to him in English, she could not speak German. 'I helped you once, help me now,' she implored him urgently.

He looked down at her manacled wrists, and decided not to know. He addressed her in German, he could not understand what she had said in English.

'I thought, I had met you once before, Fraulein, I was mistaken,' and clicking his heels together, he gave a quick Nazi salute, dismissing the shabby group, and walked away.

Her moment of brief respite was over.

Epilogue

The Embankment 1984

Susan Jones gazed at the ships passing over the Thames river, unseeingly.

The gloom on this dark November day was again descending. With a sigh she picked up her carrier bag, and prepared to leave for home. Lights were beginning to appear in the offices, car lights were trying to pierce the fog, as night began to settle in. At that moment, three boys with flashy Raleigh bicycles came into her view, riding around each other, on the pavement, stopping and starting, banging into each other, laughing. They hardly noticed Susan.

Their ages couldn't be more than nine or ten, she mused. One of them shouted to the others, 'I can't go home yet, her boyfriend will be there.'

'What about the old man,' enquired his friend. The boy was engrossed with pumping up his wheel.

'Oh, he doesn't count, no one takes notice of him.' Their voices grew fainter, as they faded into the gloom, cursing and swearing.

What a difference in this modern world, Susan thought. In my day, swearing was not heard of, now, in every sentence. 'Did they all die in vain?' she wondered, her voice echoing her thoughts, as she set out for home.

She carefully crossed the road, at the lights. The embankment was as busy as ever. She found, if she raised her umbrella above her head as she crossed, it would bring the traffic to a halt. This gave her a certain amount of satisfaction. Safe on the other side, she noticed a small church, hedged in by two larger buildings on each side, often seen in London.

She felt a strange compulsion, leading her towards the wooden entrance. It would take the weight off my feet for a while, she considered practically. A Service was taking place, it was hard to find a seat, the church was packed. She walked laboriously along the flagstoned floor, until she found an empty space in a pew.

She sat down, shutting her eyes. 'Forgive me Lord, for I have sinned,' she mouthed softly, her face was bathed in tears. 'My guilt lies heavily on me, it never leaves me.' Was it her imagination, a small voice seemed to answer her, 'Come to me, I will give you rest.'

Her attention was then caught by the minister, giving the sermon.

'Today, we will pray for our loved ones who gave their lives in world war two.' The priest continued, 'They were the small people lost in history, the peasants, railway workers, the factory workers, the nurses, the farmers, old men and women, tough as the soil they tilled.'

How strange, thought Susan, 'Why today? As if he knew my thoughts, and through my unhappiness, he would give me absolution.'

The clergyman went on, 'Without the self sacrifice, and co-operation of thousands of ordinary people during the evil years of fascism, we, the following generation, would have been enslaved ourselves, we would not be alive or free today! Let us pray.'

There was a shuffling of knees on hassocks, as the congregation bent to pray. Susan put her hand on her forehead, closing her eyes. She felt peculiarly uplifted, as if there was a reason for her being here in this church.

'The past has gone,' she heard the small voice in her head, 'Go and live in peace for evermore.'

THE END